THE DEFECTOR

The Amulet Saga
Volume Two

by

Avily Jerome

THE DEFECTOR
Published by Dragontail Press
PO Box 54550
Phoenix, AZ, 85078

ISBN 978-1-7321879-4-8
Copyright © 2017 by Avily Jerome
Cover art concept by Sarah Collotta
Cover design by Kirk DouPonce, Dog Eared Design

Available in print from your local bookstore, online, or from the author at:
www.avilyjerome.com

For more information on this book and the author visit: www.avilyjerome.com

Brought to you by Avily Jerome
And by Dragontail Press, www.avilyjerome.com

Library of Congress Cataloging-in-Publication Data
Jerome, Avily
The Silver Shores/Avily Jerome 1st ed.

Printed in the United States of America.

For Heather, my best friend.

Thank you for all your support and encouragement.

May the next nineteen years of our friendship

be as rich as the last.

Acknowledgments

Special thanks to my husband, who supports me financially and emotionally, and who allows me to pursue my passion.

Thanks also to my dad, whose continual support for my writing and my books blesses me beyond words.

Thanks to my mom, who taught me to read and instilled in me an endless love of the written word.

And, of course, thank you to my readers, the ones who are still interested in what's going on in Legerdemain

Table of Contents

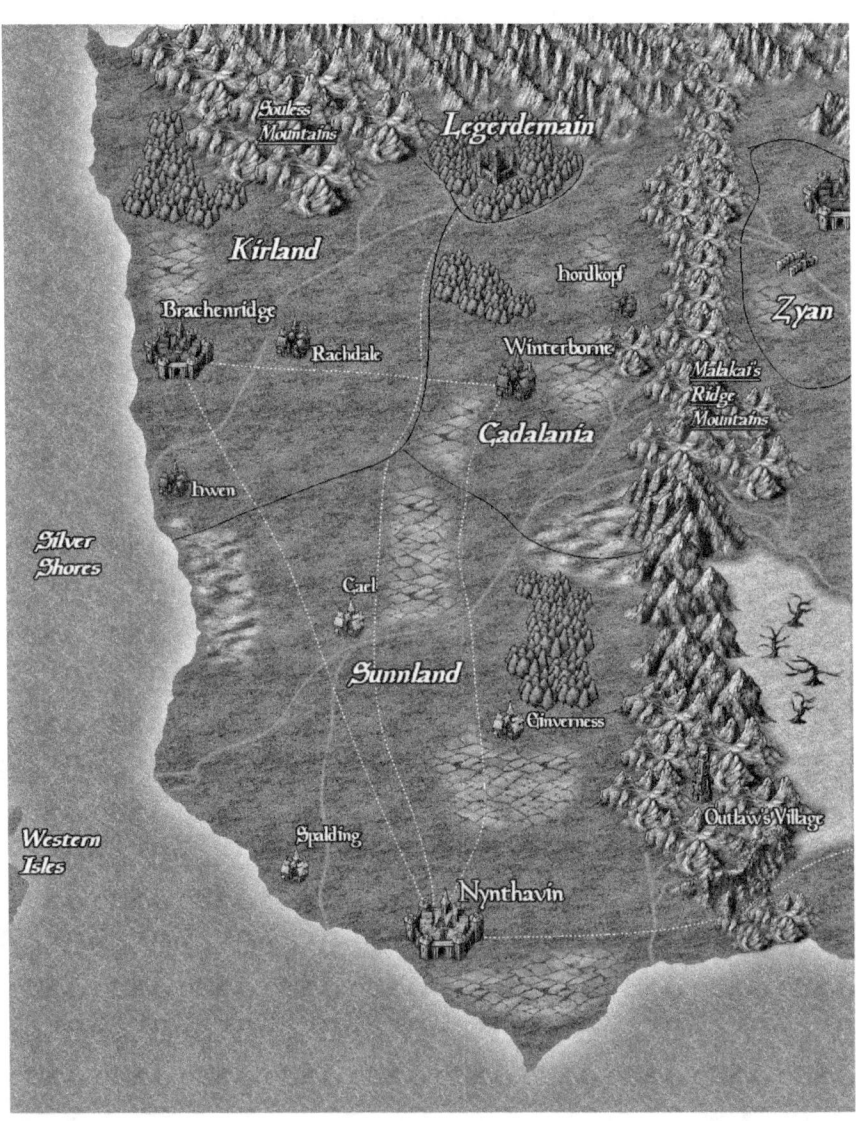

The daughter of the dragon
Who oversees the land
Will live until the day
The dragons come again

Love she'll never know
A child she'll never have
The kings and queens of fate
Her legacy will show

From the path fate strays
The Lover and the Traitor
When the Solstice Moon shines brightly
And at the Dragon, the Dancer waves

Across the ocean wide
The darkness rises swiftly
Untold power unleashed
Building until that day

The reign of power shifts
Fate in the balance
The weight of choices made
Brings life or the end of all

The child lost arises
To take the power back
A child of the enemy
Begotten then to conquer

When the dragons rise again
When the mountains open wide
When the stones of heaven fall
The world is remade.

When the darkness reigns
Then the hate shall bind
The hearts of one and all
Until the light is found

Those who triumph fall
Those who seek shall find
Those who rule shall serve
The servant, ruler of all

The begotten of the dragons
Beloved of the Creator
Who bears the Dragon Stone
The Deliverer of the World

THE DEFECTOR

The Amulet Saga
Volume Two

Seeing

"Sight is a gift. It cannot be learned," Ada said.

Princess Anarosia watched carefully as Ada prepared the bowl.

"I can teach you the sequence," Ada went on, "but Seeing is never a guarantee."

Anarosia settled at the table and lit the candle. Sight was the one element of magic Ada hadn't spent much time on when teaching Anarosia her lessons. "It's foolish to try to know the future, and it rarely plays out how you think it will, even if you do see a glimpse," she always said. But Anarosia insisted on at least trying.

She focused, exactly as Ada had shown her, gazing into the bowl. She felt with her mind for the magic that permeated the air and drew it in, drawing it through her mind and into the bowl of herbs and water.

A picture formed. Herself, on the throne. She and her brother, in an argument. She couldn't hear the words, but somehow she knew he was questioning her judgment, saying she was not the woman he remembered, saying she wasn't fit to be queen.

She saw herself sign edicts, ones that made no sense, giving over power to foreign lands. She was cruel to servants, haughty before Parliament, angry at everyone who challenged her.

Her mother and brothers begged for her to be reasonable, but she ignored them. Then for no reason she could discern, she ordered their deaths. All of them, hanged.

The vision faded and Anarosia sat up, gasping.

Such a thing couldn't be true. She would never do those things. Could never do them. The vision was false. A mistake, somehow.

But Seeing was never wrong. It showed the future. Wasn't that what she wanted?

"What did you See?" Ada asked.

Anarosia blinked. "I... nothing. It didn't work."

Ada raised an eyebrow. Of course, she must know Anarosia was lying, but she didn't press the issue.

"You'd best get back, then. Your father will be wondering where you are."

That afternoon, in the council meeting, it was all Anarosia could do to keep her mind focused on the matters of state they discussed. Every glance from her brother, every nod, every expression, every word he spoke that contradicted hers, seemed ominous, laden with meaning. Would he say something to be deserving of his fate?

But of course he wouldn't.

There had to be another explanation for her vision. It couldn't really mean that her kingdom would suffer with her as queen, could it? There had to be another option.

That night, she prepared a bowl with the herbs the way Ada had showed her, and focused on Seeing. The vision reappeared, only this time it showed even more of her deeds. Deaths at her hands, the country becoming destitute.

There was something... odd about her appearance in the vision. She was plumper than she was now, prettier somehow, though she couldn't quite determine why. Her mannerisms seemed off, but she didn't know what had caused the change. Something was wrong. Could it be she was enjoying her power, reveling in a dictatorship, growing fat on the backs of her people?

The vision faded and she went to bed, pondering its meaning, but she could find no way out. She dreamed of it again, during one of the many snatches of sleep she managed to get that night.

A short rap at the door woke her from the dream just as she saw herself putting a man to death for what seemed to be a minor offense.

"Enter," she called.

Her maid, Myrta, came in. Myrta's mouth opened in a silent gasp. "M'lady, are you ill?" She rushed to Anarosia's bedside and pressed a hand to her forehead.

"I'm fine, I just couldn't sleep well last night."

Myrta set Anarosia's breakfast tray on the table beside her and tucked the blankets around her. "You must go back to sleep, then. I'll inform your father that you're unwell."

Anarosia shook her head. "No, that won't cure me. I just need to think."

Myrta eyed her, but didn't protest. "You will let me know how I can be of service, m'lady? I will do anything to help."

Anarosia smiled. "I will let you know if I think of anything. Thank you, Myrta."

Myrta was a good servant. Loyal and trustworthy. Maybe she could tell Myrta about the vision. Maybe… But not yet.

Clouds

Ada scrutinized the princess. Dark circles lined her eyes. Her fingernails, once long and elegant, were short and jagged from being chewed. Her eagerness for learning had waned to a dull listlessness.

Ada had seen this sort of thing before. Experienced it herself more often than she cared to admit. This was the danger in knowing too much.

She followed Anarosia to her room and closed the door with a bang.

The princess jumped. "Ada. I didn't see you come in."

"What did you See?"

Anarosia's face went pale. Paler than usual. "I... what do you mean?"

Ada crossed her arms over her chest, the way she'd done when Anarosia was a child, committing some infraction of the rules. "You lied to me about what you Saw before, and then you tried Seeing again. Without me there to guide you."

"I know better than to try that level of magic without an instructor," Anarosia said.

"And yet you did it, and you Saw something you can't interpret." Ada hobbled to the bed and sat down, patting the mattress beside her. "Tell me what it is."

Anarosia sighed and sat down. "I saw my future, and I don't like who I become."

Ada frowned. "Do not be so certain of the future. Seeing gives us a glimpse into what will be. But be cautious. What you think you See may not be an accurate interpretation of what will be."

She patted Anarosia's leg, then stood. "Don't make any rash decisions based on an incomplete picture."

She ambled from the room, but the conversation lingered. What had the girl Seen, to have shaken her so? Anarosia was bright and loving. Self-sacrificing to a fault. She'd always been eager to fulfill her role as queen, and promised to be a good one. What could cause her to doubt herself so much?

Ada made her way down the long, winding stairs to her chambers and readied her supplies. Even in all her years working magic, Seeing still caused her heart to race. There was a reason she'd instructed Anarosia—and countless pupils before her—never to attempt it without her to guide them.

The future, in all its twists and possibilities, followed certain pre-ordained paths, and knowing those paths had been the undoing of many great men and women. Seeing always showed the unalterable future. What was Seen could not be changed or undone.

However, events rarely fell out as expected. The visions themselves, though incomplete, were always accurate, but out of context it was nearly impossible to tell what reality would be. It was only after they transpired that what was Seen really made sense.

Ada lit her candle and mixed her herbs, then drew on the natural energies that surrounded her.

A vision formed in her bowl, then another.

Two possible futures.

In all her years, Ada had never seen a future that wasn't set.

She focused on the two paths.

In each, Anarosia made a choice, though Ada couldn't see what those choices would be.

In the first, the dire future Anarosia had seen would come to pass. Ada couldn't See exactly what would happen—circumstances and details were gray and blurry—she could only sense that Anarosia had good reason to fear it.

Times would be dark for many years before they were put right again.

In the other possible future, the decision Anarosia made would avoid this darkness. Anarosia would have a future of serenity and peace,

15

and die happy when she was old. But something far worse would come later. A darkness so consuming, it sent tremors reverberating through Ada's old bones. In the second future, beyond Anarosia's life and rule, Ada saw her own death, and the utter destruction of the entire kingdom. In the first future, the darkness would still come, but there was hope. Hope that the evil could be overcome. Something about the choice Anarosia made would determine whether or not the kingdom could be saved.

Ada emerged from the vision, sweating and trembling, but impressed with two unchangeable truths. First, a dark time was destined to come upon the kingdom of Legerdemain. Anarosia's decision would now would ultimately spell the salvation or destruction of Legerdemain.

Second, it was a choice only Anarosia could make. She could sacrifice her own happiness for the future of the kingdom, or she could live her life in tranquility and happiness, and ultimately doom her kingdom.

The worst part of having Seen, however, of knowing the possibilities and their outcomes, was that Ada didn't know which choice was which. The choice that seemed right might end up being wrong, and the choice which seemed self-sacrificing might end up the selfish one. The two paths twisted and intertwined, and the cloud surrounding them both was so murky, Ada couldn't see what the choices were, let alone which was the right one, either for Anarosia or for the future of Legerdemain. She couldn't give counsel, couldn't help. She could only wait, and hope Anarosia chose the right one.

Loyalty

"Let me help with that." Anarosia took the other end of the coverlet her servant Myrta was shaking out the window.

"Really, m'lady, you shouldn't. It's unbecoming of the crown princess."

"Since when has that bothered me?"

Myrta smiled. "Very well, but if your mother walks in, don't say I didn't warn you."

"If my mother walks in, we'll say we were designing a new cape for the next ball."

Myrta giggled.

The two finished shaking the coverlet and Anarosia helped spread it over her bed. She sighed. "They fill my head with politics and battle tactics and etiquette, but I can't even make a bed. I wonder if that's…" she stopped and sighed again.

"Something is troubling you, ml'lady?"

A flash of the vision she'd Seen imprinted itself on her mind. "Do you think people change, Myrta?" Can someone just wake up and find they're the opposite of who they thought they were, who they ever wanted to be?"

"I don't know, m'lady. It might seem so to someone else, if the person was especially good at hiding his true self. But I think you know, deep inside, who you are. It would take a very significant event—a spell or a betrayal, perhaps—to make you change that deeply within."

The door opened and the queen swept in. "Anarosia, what are you doing?"

"Myrta and I were inspired by this pattern, and we were discussing how it might translate into a pattern for a new cape. Perhaps for a dinner or ball."

The queen's lovely features relaxed into a smile. "That sounds like a charming idea. I'll send the seamstress up after lunch to hear your ideas. But come, there is a dignitary here from Kirland. She has agreed to teach you some of their customs so you'll know how to behave should you ever find yourself there."

Anarosia smiled at Myrta, who covered her mouth with her hands to stifle a giggle.

Anarosia sat politely through her international customs lesson, but her mind kept returning to her vision. What would it take for her to become like her vision? A spell or a betrayal, Myrta had suggested. Not a spell. That wasn't how magic worked. Magic was from nature, as much as trees of flowers or air. It could affect those things, and it could be used to change things, even the way things appeared, but it couldn't change who someone was at their core.

A betrayal, then?

Who would betray her so grievously that she'd turn into the monster she'd seen?

Or perhaps nothing would happen, but her fear that it would was what would cause her to become paranoid and insane, and it was she herself who created the future she saw.

She gripped her skirt in her fists. There had to be a way to prevent it, to change it somehow.

The Kirish woman stopped talking and looked at Anarosia.

Anarosia stood and clasped the woman's hand. "Thank you so much. This has been very informative. Will you be staying for the ball?"

"Yes, but I'll be leaving shortly after that."

"It has been lovely having you visit. Please, let me know if you need any assistance with your gown or anything else."

"Thank you, Your Highness."

Anarosia escorted the dignitary back to the suite she'd been given for her visit, then headed back toward her study.

Outside the library, she was nearly run over by a young man racing down the corridor.

"Amberte, what are you doing?"

Anarosia's younger brother gasped. I'm supposed to be practicing my writing, but I've lost my royal seal. Father will have my hide. I can't find it anywhere, and I'm late."

Anarosia smiled. He was nearly a man, but sometimes still acted like a child. Such came from being the youngest, she supposed. She slipped the seal ring off her finger and handed it to her brother. "Take mine. But you must find yours as soon as your lesson is over."

"I will. I promise. Thank you, Ana!"

The boy dashed off back the way he'd come, past Ada, who stood in a little alcove.

Anarosia smiled and curtsied.

"You don't think that's a bit risky?"

Anarosia shook her head. "He's always losing something or another. It will turn up. And if it doesn't, I'll say I lost mine."

"He'll never learn responsibility if you always hide his mistakes."

Anarosia laughed. "Did anyone ever warn you of that when you covered up mine?"

The old woman smiled, but her keen eyes studied Anarosia.

Anarosia's laugh turned sour in her mouth as a memory of the vision flashed before her.

Amberte, older, handsome, led away in chains, accused of treason. Ordered to his death. Ordered by Anarosia.

She choked back a shudder and smiled. "I must get back to work on my own lessons. Good day."

She could feel Ada's eyes on her as she swept down the hall. The old woman had been advisor, midwife, and friend for longer than Anarosia knew. Behind that withered face was a mind that held the wisdom of generations.

Anarosia always felt as though Ada knew far more than she let on. Could she see the struggle Anarosia felt? The future she feared? Did she know the atrocities Anarosia would commit against a young man to whom she'd once given her own signet ring to save him from punishment?

Anarosia made it back to her chamber and closed the door, leaning against it for support, her own studies relegated to an afterthought.

She couldn't stay here, constantly wondering what horrors lay just out of sight, betrayals or treasonous plots that would cause her to destroy everything she loved most. She couldn't become the person she Saw.

Ada always said the future couldn't be changed. That was one reason why Seeing was so dangerous. But Anarosia had to try. She'd do anything to keep that future from coming to pass.

"You're distressed again, m'lady."

Anarosia jumped at the sound of her servant's voice. "Myrta! I didn't see you there."

"I apologize, m'lady. I didn't mean to startle you. I just meant... It troubles me to see you so upset. It is my duty to help you, and if you're upset, I fear I have failed you."

Anarosia smiled. "Dear Myrta. What troubles me is out of either of our control."

Myrta smiled. "You will let me know if there's anything I can do to help?"

Anarosia looked at her, really seeing her for perhaps the first time. She wasn't much older than Anarosia. And she was beautiful. And kind. She spent all her time meeting Anarosia's needs—did she even have time for a life of her own?

"Do you have a beau, Myrta?"

Myrta blinked. "Pardon me?"

"A lover. A special someone. Do you even have time to do anything for yourself?"

Myrta opened and closed her mouth a few times before answering. "My place is with you, m'lady. I have never wanted anything but to serve you." She sounded as though she really meant it.

An idea wormed its way into Anarosia's mind. "Myrta, can I trust you?"

"With your life, m'lady."

"There is something I must do, but I can't do it alone. It would require your complete discretion and silence."

"You have it, as always."

"I need to leave Legerdemain. I can't explain why, but I must go and no one can know about it."

Myrta's eyes widened. "Leave? For how long?"

"I don't know. Maybe forever."

"But... you're to be the queen."

"I won't be when I leave. I'll be just another woman, making my way in the world. But I'll need you to help me plan my escape."

Myrta nodded. "Of course I will help you. When will we go?"

"Oh, Myrta, I didn't mean… I couldn't ask you to come with me. I will have no home, no livelihood. I don't know how far I will have to travel. I wouldn't dream of asking you to give up your home and your life to come with me."

"As I said, m'lady, my place is with you. I have no lover, no one to leave behind, no one to care if I'm gone. You have my loyalty, to the end of the world. When do we leave?"

Escape

Rose pulled her violet cloak around her shoulders. She glanced both ways as she left her chambers to make sure no one was watching, and headed down the corridor toward the stable.

"Anarosia, darling, are you going somewhere?"

Rose's heart stuttered. She turned to face her mother.

Mother glided along the marble floor, looking immaculate in her blue silk gown, with her hair pulled smoothly back into a bun behind her diadem.

"I'm going to the South Village, remember? Father wanted me to meet with the merchants."

"Oh, just look at your hair. Did your maid lose your brush? You can't go out looking like that."

Rose tucked a strand of hair behind her ear, not that it mattered. A dozen more stuck out in every direction. It didn't matter how many times Myrta brushed it or how many pins she used to secure it, within minutes, it always frayed and fell.

Mother stroked Rose's cheek. "Have you been using the potion Ada made for your freckles?"

"I don't need a potion to get rid of my freckles, Mother. They're fine where they are." She toyed with the edge of her cloak, hoping her mother wouldn't sense her anxiety.

Mother sighed. "I don't know what to do with you sometimes. Come along, your father wants a word with you."

Rose clenched her fists. She was so close. But she had to maintain the illusion of normalcy.

She followed her mother toward the throne room. Two guards stood by the door. They bowed and opened the door as Mother swept toward them.

Rose followed closely behind. She curtsied before her father. "You asked to see me?"

Father nodded. "I want you to stay here and let your brother deal with the merchants."

No. No, this could *not* be happening.

She took a deep breath to maintain her composure. "I see. Why?"

"Well, because... because he's..."

"Male?"

Father sputtered, but didn't deny it.

"I am two years his senior, and I am to be queen one day. If you cannot trust me even to negotiate with the traders, how can you trust me to lead the kingdom?"

"I've been discussing with Parliament..."

"You can't undo hundreds of years of law and tradition because you think men are smarter or more capable," Rose said, her tone beginning to indicate her feelings. "I've studied our history, and we've had as many good queens as kings. And bad, as well. The law says that the throne passes to the firstborn, and I intend to be as good a queen as any before me." Ironic, that she fought so hard for a job she didn't want. The principle stood, anyway.

"The girl speaks wisdom."

Rose jumped. She hadn't even noticed the old woman sitting in the corner by the tapestry that hung behind the king's throne.

Ada looked at her with such intensity, Rose felt like the woman's eyes burned a hole right through her.

Rose turned away and faced her father again. "If I fail, you can send Andro to clean up whatever disaster I create."

"Oh, Anarosia, don't be so dramatic." Mother waved her hand, as though to wave away Rose's theatrics like a bad smell.

Rose frowned. This was partly her mother's fault. Father married a wealthy beauty who had no ambition beyond thwarting the ravages of time for as long as possible.

"This is my duty, Father. Let me fulfill it."

Father let out a long sigh. "Very well. Make sure you cover all the points we discussed, especially regarding fair trade for Legerdemain amethysts."

"I'll remember."

"Make sure you have enough gold," Ada said from her perch by the tapestry.

Rose looked at her. The old woman smiled and winked.

What did she know? And how did she know it?

"Yes, of course," Father said. He called for his treasurer and ordered a chest of gold coins to be brought. "Make sure you take enough guards to protect yourself and my gold."

"I will be safe," Rose promised.

"Be back in time to get ready for dinner," Mother said. "I invited a potential suitor for you to meet."

Rose bit the inside of her cheek to keep from saying anything inappropriate. "Yes, Mother."

She turned and hurried toward the stable before she could get stalled any more.

The guard carrying the gold stumbled along behind her, struggling to keep up carrying the heavy chest.

Myrta, waited with two horses.

"Is everything in order?" Rose asked.

Myrta glanced at the guard before nodding and curtsying. "Yes, m'lady."

"Have another horse saddled," Rose ordered.

She turned to the guard. "Help me put the gold in the saddlebags. It will be best if the merchants don't know how much we have."

The guard obeyed, and by the time his horse was saddled, the gold was distributed between Rose and Myrta.

Almost an hour later, they arrived at the sprawling merchant's estate on the edge of the South Village.

"Stay here and guard the gold," Rose ordered the guard.

She swept into the courtyard and was met by a servant.

"Right this way, madam," he said, leading her inside.

The troupe of merchants sat around a table, eating.

The man at the head of the table stood. "Good afternoon, m'lady. I received your letter. It is an honor to receive a visit from the leader of the merchant's guild, of course, although I was given to understand that I'd be dealing with the princess herself."

26

"As I stated in my letter, the king decided it would be better to have a first-hand account of the merchant trade and practices. As the leader of the merchant's guild, it is my duty to accompany you. My second and I will verify imports and prices and fair trade value for the imports being brought into our nation."

"Yes, Lady Rose," the merchant said. "We are prepared to leave on your command."

"Very good. We leave within the hour."

The merchants scrambled to prepare to leave.

Once they were busy, Rose went out to where Myrta and the guard waited. "Negotiations are starting well, but I forgot my signet ring, so I cannot formalize anything." She looked at the guard. "You must retrieve it for me. We have a lot of work ahead yet, so take your time. And please, apologize to my Mother for me, as I might not make it back in time for dinner."

The guard began the trip back toward the castle and Rose took Myrta's hand. "You have our things?"

Myrta nodded. "Waiting at the tavern. I'll go get them immediately."

Rose smiled. "It worked perfectly. My family has no idea what we're doing, and the merchants believed my story. By the time the guard gets back, we'll be out of the kingdom and on our way to freedom."

The Road

Rose inhaled deeply, reveling in the new sights and smells. "Isn't it beautiful here?"

Myrta sneezed. "I don't know about beautiful. It's too flat. It isn't natural to be able to see so far without seeing any trees or mountains."

The forest that encircled Legerdemain had passed out of view more than a week past. Rose and Myrta parted from the caravan two days before. It was only a matter of time before Rose's father's soldiers caught up to the caravan, and she wanted to be as far in the opposite direction as possible before that happened.

While the caravan made its way south and east toward Cadalania, she and Myrta traveled south and west toward Sunnland, the largest and most prosperous kingdom this side of Malakai's Ridge. Best of all, no one in the caravan knew she was gone. She and Myrta slipped away at the last village, a small town that gave its allegiance and taxes to Kirland, telling conflicting stories of which part of the caravan they'd be riding with that day. No one in the caravan would miss them for at least a day. If Rose had calculated correctly, that would be about the time her father's guards caught up. By the time all the confusion was sorted out, she and Myrta would be another day or two away, and they'd be lost in the bustle of the city long before anyone picked up their trail.

"At least we're not going east," Myrta said. "I've heard the desert is nothing but sand for days and days."

Rose shuddered. "I don't know that the sea will be much better. Water in all directions for days sounds just as bad."

"I've always wanted to travel the sea. Perhaps we could sail to the Silver Shores. Didn't one of your ancestors live there?"

"A great uncle, I believe. But I don't think he'd recommend it. However, we don't need to go across the sea. I'm sure there will be plenty of opportunity for work in a city like Nynthavin."

"I do hope you're right, m'lady."

"Rose. You must call me Rose. We're equals, now."

Myrta snorted, but didn't argue.

By late afternoon, Rose's back ached from sitting so long in the saddle, and her backside ached even more, though it was better than it had been the first few days, yet the landscape stretched on, low rolling hills in every direction, with not so much as a farmhouse in sight, let alone a village.

"Surely we must be almost to the sea by now," Myrta said.

Rose frowned. Everything looked so much closer together on the maps she'd studied. She knew Legerdemain was small—she could travel from one end to the other in a day—but she hadn't realized how large the rest of the world really was.

Night fell, and darkness obscured the road. Rose urged the horses to pick up their pace, but they were weary, too.

"I suppose we'll have to camp under the stars tonight," Rose said at last.

Myrta nodded "At this point, I'd sleep anywhere."

A small cluster of bushes grew a little off the side of the road. "How about there?" Rose suggested.

They dismounted and tethered the horses to the bushes.

"Should we build a fire?" Myrta asked.

"I don't know how," Rose confessed.

Myrta frowned. "I could do it in a fireplace, but I've never tried outside."

"Let's not, then. At least it's warmer here than at home."

Rose spread her cloak on the ground and pulled some provisions from her saddlebags. "We'll have to buy more food at the next village. I didn't think we'd be traveling this long."

They ate in relative silence.

The sound of hooves on the road broke the stillness. Rose's heart thundered louder than the horse. Could it be her father's guards, coming to take her home?

A lone rider ambled up the road. He wasn't wearing a Legerdemain guard uniform, but that didn't mean he wasn't sent for her.

Not that it mattered. It was too late to run away and there was no place to hide.

The man rode on.

Just when Rose thought he might pass by without stopping, he veered toward them and waved. "Greetings, ladies. I was looking for a good place to stay the night. This seems just the place. If you'll accept my company, of course."

Rose didn't recognize him, which meant he most likely wasn't sent for her.

She smiled. "We would be delighted. I am Rose, and this is Myrta."

The man dismounted and tethered his horse near theirs. "I am Sir Billham of Kirland."

A gentleman. Her relief was almost palpable. "We are from…" Rose tried to remember what would be far away from Kirland but still a probable location for them to be traveling from. "Zyan. We're from Zyan."

"Oh, artisans, then?"

Rose nodded. "On our way to Nynthavin, looking for work. Have you traveled this way before? Do you know how much further it is?"

"Oh, not too much more, now. On horseback, you can make it in a week, though ten days is more realistic. Fortunately, the villages are closer together the closer you get to the city."

Another whole week? Rose's heart sank. Every day they were out in the open gave her father's men that much more opportunity to find her. Still, all they could do was press on.

They talked for awhile longer, Sir Billham regaling them with tales of his travels, and then Rose and Myrta curled up in their cloaks to sleep.

Rose woke up sometime before dawn to the sound of a yelp from Myrta. She sat up. Dark forms wrestled in the dark. The bigger one landed a blow to the smaller one's face. Myrta cried out again. The other shadow—Sir Billham, apparently—sprang up and mounted his horse. He bolted for the road. Rose's horse, and Myrta's, followed.

No, not followed. Were led away.

Rose ran after them, but they were gone in moments. She hurried back to Myrta, whose once-fine dress was now stained with a growing patch of blood from her nose. "Oh, Myrta. I am so sorry."

"I am the one who is sorry, m'lady. I couldn't stop him. He took everything. The saddlebags, the horses..." Myrta choked. She looked up at Rose. "What do we do now?"

Beggars

Rose stared down the dusty road in the direction the thief had gone until long after the sun climbed over the hills to the east. Myrta sat beside her, silent for a long while.

At last, Myrta put a hand on Rose's arm. "What do you want to do now, m'lady?"

Rose choked back the tears that clouded her eyes and lodged in her throat. "I don't know. He took our money and our clothes and even our food. I suppose we must go home. But I don't even know how to get there without a horse. It's been days since the last village, even on horseback. We'll starve before we get anywhere. And there's no telling how long it will be before my father's men come this way. We can't just sit and wait to be rescued, either."

Myrta stood and brushed the dust from her backside. "Very well, then. If we cannot go back and we cannot stay here, we must move forward. Come along. There's no time to waste." She reached a hand down to Rose.

Rose grabbed it and heaved herself up. She stood in the road, staring in the way the thief had gone, while Myrta picked up both their cloaks and shook the dust from them.

Myrta handed Rose her cloak. "You still have the amethyst clasp. If need be, you could sell it."

Rose nodded, only half listening. She glanced back the way they had come, half hoping to see a dust cloud announcing her father's soldiers. If they came, some of them could return her home, while the others went in search of Sir Billham, the thief.

But no cloud of dust appeared, and Myrta was already walking down the road, continuing toward Nynthavin.

Rose followed. There wasn't really anything else to do.

By afternoon, sweat and dirt caked every inch of her. Her body ached in places she didn't know existed. She'd taken off her dainty riding boots when the blisters that wore away at her feet became raw and started to bleed, and now she stepped carefully over the road in torn stockings.

"Rose, look."

Rose straightened her weary back and looked through the dusty glare to where Myrta pointed. "What is that?"

"I believe it's a farmhouse. Come on. At the least they will give us some water." Myrta pressed forward, not seeming to be nearly as weary and sore as Rose.

Rose followed, straining with every step.

Myrta knocked on the farmhouse door. A young woman, not much older than Rose, with a baby on her hip and a toddler hiding behind her legs, opened it.

"Greetings, good woman," Myrta said. "My companion and I were travelling to Nynthavin and were set upon by thieves. They took everything we had, down to our food and water. Do you perhaps have something we could eat and drink? We will gladly help with any chores in exchange for whatever you can spare."

The woman nodded. She pointed to a stone cistern a little way from the house. "Help yourself to some water. I'll bring you some meat and bread."

Myrta bowed. "Thank you, kind lady."

Myrta led the way to the cistern and drew a dipper of water. She handed it to Rose. Rose gulped it down, splashing it on her face and chest in the process. Myrta continued to dip and hand Rose water until Rose was satisfied, then drank some herself.

A few minutes later, the farm woman emerged, without her children, and handed Myrta a parcel. "There is some meat and bread and cheese, there. You are welcome to it. I don't need any help with chores."

Myrta bowed. "You are kind and gracious. We thank you heartily for your hospitality. Could I trouble you to tell me how far it is to the next village?"

"You can reach it by nightfall, if you hurry," the farm woman said.

Myrta nodded. "Our thanks again. May the Creator bless you."

The woman raised an eyebrow, as though that was an unfamiliar phrase to her, but nodded. "Best of luck. May the goddess guide your way."

Myrta took one more sip of water, then pulled Rose along back to the road.

"She could've at least let us stay and rest a bit," Rose grumbled.

Myrta shook her head. "She was smart. She has a home and a family to protect. She doesn't know us. Doesn't know if our story is any truer than Sir Billham's. She didn't invite us in, and she didn't give us any excuse to stay. She'll watch us until we're out of sight, and she'll be wary for the next few days, but her family will be safe. And she fed us and gave us water. She did more than we can fairly expect. We're beggars now, Rose, and until your father comes for us, we must behave like it."

Myrta opened the parcel and handed Rose a thick chunk of soft bread. It was almost the best thing Rose had ever tasted. She tore off big bites and swallowed them, hardly chewing in her haste to devour as much as possible. Myrta then handed her some meat and cheese, eating some herself while they walked.

Just as darkness settled over the land, Myrta pointed to a light in the distance, at the base of the next hill. "That must be the village. Come on, Rose. We can rest soon."

One light turned to two, and soon a handful of them glittered in the valley before them. As they walked, the lights became windows, and the windows nestled in buildings.

"A house. Perhaps we can get help there," Rose said as they approached the first building.

Myrta shook her head. "Follow my lead, m'lady."

Rose nodded. She was too tired to object.

Myrta walked to the green in the center of the village. The road circled it, and shops lined the road on the other side. Myrta paused and looked at the signs before continuing.

"This way." Myrta walked toward a two-story inn called the Wayward Peddler.

Rose followed her around the side of the building to a back door that stood open, revealing a hot, fragrant kitchen.

Myrta knocked. A robust woman in a stained apron came to the door, and Myrta told her the same story she'd told the farm woman.

The woman nodded. "Come on in. I can spare a morsel to eat. One of our regular girls is sick and didn't come in tonight, so you can serve in the tavern to earn your dinner and a place to sleep if you like."

Myrta bowed. "We would be most grateful. I fear we have nothing suitable to wear, however."

The woman eyed their once-fine garments.

"As you can see," Myrta said, "our clothes are worth quite a lot once they're clean. A person might get a small fortune for them if a trader came by. We would be willing to part with our gowns in exchange for a few days' wages and some more sensible clothes."

The woman rubbed her chin. "I'll see if anyone is interested. I do have some extra dresses you can wear for tonight, at any rate."

She led them to a back storage room and handed them each a coarse brown dress and stained apron.

"Come on," Myrta urged as soon as the door shut them in. She handed Rose some of the food left from the farm woman. "We can eat more and sleep as soon as we do some work."

When they were changed, Myrta put their cloaks in a burlap bag with the rest of the food from the farm woman and tucked the bag in the corner of the store room. "I'm hoping she won't think of the cloaks when she gets the gowns. Above all, we must keep the amethyst safe." She looked at Rose. "Are you ready to begin your new life as a tavern maid?"

Bandit

Taurin slid his sword blade along the stone in slow, deliberate strokes. Shards of light reflected off the specks of mica in the surrounding rocks. Taurin adjusted the turban shading his eyes and scooted a little closer to the rock that sheltered him. From his position partway up the mountain, he could see the desert sprawled before him, seemingly endless sand and withered, prickly plants.

The caravan was due that day, but it couldn't get to his location from the city before midday.

The sun beat down, climbing higher, shrinking his patch of shade. Far in the distance, a dust cloud formed along the road.

Taurin whistled a long, sharp note. His crew slithered out of the crack in the rocks that led to the camp, like the lizards that lived there, creeping down to join him behind the boulders that lined the pass.

"Guards will be at the front and the rear," he said. "So we strike at the middle. Teams of two, take what you can carry and get away."

He eyed the two newest members of his band, men who had left the mercenary guild from the last caravan, hoping for a bigger payday. "We're not going for the whole caravan, and we're trying to avoid casualties. If you kill people, they send soldiers after you. Take what you can and meet back at the camp to divide. Everyone understand?"

The group nodded their affirmation.

"Gill, you take Winnet, and Jyn, you take Barbo. Show 'em how we do things."

Jyn's eyes seemed to get even blacker than usual as she glared at him, but he knew she'd obey. She didn't look it, with her wiry frame and delicate features, but she would have no trouble keeping the newcomer in line.

Soon, the sounds of horses and wagons could be heard, growing louder as the caravan drew closer.

A few riders broke away from the group and rode ahead as they neared the pass.

Mercenary guards.

Taurin waved his hand toward Crow to bring the two horses that waited behind a large rock. Taking the narrow path between rocks and cliffs, Taurin and Crow headed toward the narrowest part of the pass, while Maury and Donnin, who'd been with him long enough to know what to do, went ahead, just around the bend.

A few moments later, the two riders came around the corner.

Taurin and Crow rode into the road, blocking the mercenaries' path.

"Ho!" the first guard hollered, reining his horse.

Crow charged, swinging a club at the first rider. The horse reared and the rider fell off. Crow rode toward the next rider while Taurin grabbed the reins of the first horse and pulled it toward the narrow path leading into the mountains.

Crow would get the other one, leaving both mercenaries wounded, to be picked up when the caravan reached that point. That would slow them enough for the rest of the band to attack.

Taurin reached the edge of the path into the rocks. His horse reared, as did the horse he led. He clung to the horse's neck, and looked around for what had spooked it. He looked up just as someone dropped on him from the top of the boulder to his left.

Another mercenary. How had he...

Taurin's head hit the ground with a crack as the mercenary crashed on top of him.

How had they known? Taurin chose a different location each time. The mountain pass went on for miles, but the mercenary was in the exact spot he'd picked.

He threw a punch at the mercenary on top of him and rolled out from beneath him. They tumbled over one another, rolling, scrapping, along the dusty trail.

Figures emerged from between the rocks.

37

Hundreds of them.

A whole mercenary army.

And they hadn't come that day—he'd been on watch all morning—which meant they had to have been waiting all night.

A few yards away, Crow went down, a spear through his chest.

Taurin rolled to his feet and pulled his sword. He slashed through the mercenary who'd attacked him and charged at the next one.

The first wagon of the caravan came around the bend, then the second.

His band emerged from the rocks.

"Retreat," Taurin screamed.

It was too late. Mercenaries poured from the wagons, swarming over his band.

A pair of knives flew through the air, and two of the mercenaries went down. That meant Maury. Taurin had taught him that move. The boy was alive—for now, at least.

"Keep going!" Taurin shouted, though it was unlikely anyone heard him.

Taurin slashed his way toward the path, dodging mercenaries. A spear caught him in the side, but he kept going, leaving a trail of blood in his wake.

His horse waited partway up the path, whinnying and stamping. He swung himself up and urged the animal up the steep, rocky trail at a pace that was not entirely safe.

"Taurin!"

Jyn's voice

He turned, just in time to see a spear flying toward him.

It caught him in the shoulder.

Jyn ran toward the mercenary who'd thrown it, leaping across the tops of boulders, knife in hand. She slashed wildly. "Go, Taurin," she screeched, plunging her knife into the mercenary's chest.

Taurin went. He didn't have a choice—his horse fled, and he didn't have the strength to stop it.

Two more mercenaries went after Jyn, but he didn't see the outcome of the fight. His horse carried him out of view.

Blood seeped down, soaking his clothes, and the sun leached all his energy. By the time the horse stopped running, he could barely lift his head.

The horse slowed to a meander. Taurin glanced through the sweat that stung his eyes. Nothing but desert, stretching on for miles.

His strength gave out. He tumbled from the horse, landing face-up on the hot sand. He closed his eyes against the glare.

His mind felt hazy, like the heat that shimmered in the air.

Someone had betrayed him. Warned the caravan he was going to strike. But who?

He couldn't think about it now. Not when he was so tired. He'd figure it out when he woke up.

Nightmares

Rose sat straight up, her eyes frantically searching the dark room. Sweat clung to her hair and the back of her neck, sticking in the stifling room. She gasped in a breath of stale air that smelled vaguely of moldy vegetables and spilled ale. Slowly, she started to remember where she was. The storage room in the back of the little inn.

The rough threads of the thin blanket covering the hard pallet she and Myrta shared scratched her skin, but her mind was still back home. The vision she'd had when she'd tried Seeing replayed itself over and over, growing progressively worse, night after night.

Herself, on the throne, wearing the royal crown. Looking beautiful, regal… yet somehow different. Prouder. Colder. Crueler.

She saw royal edicts, signed by her own hand, forging treaties with other nations, giving them power over her tiny land, only to have them betray her and take advantage of her. She increased taxes to meet the demands put upon her by the nations who were supposed to be her allies. Sent men into the mountains to excavate tapped-out mines in search of gemstones that weren't there, only to have them perish in the attempt, leaving their families destitute.

Everything she'd learned about government, about being a fair and gentle ruler—her future self utterly disregarded all the lessons ingrained upon her. What happened? The vision never explained how she went from being herself to being the monster she saw in the future.

What was it Ada had said? "Seeing gives us a glimpse into what will be. But be cautious—what you think you See may not be an accurate interpretation of what will be."

Yet Rose couldn't deny the truth of what she Saw. Whatever occurred in her future to cause her to be the ruin of her own kingdom, she had to try to prevent it. She could not stay if that was the ruler she was to become.

Ada said her vision was a glimpse of what would be, not what might be, but Rose had to try. She had to get far enough away that she could never do the things she foresaw.

At first, she thought it had worked. The visions that plagued her ever since the first Seeing faded, growing less frequent and less horrifying when she left the borders of Legerdemain, and for a while she'd felt free.

About a week after she'd been robbed and she and Myrta had been forced to work at the inn, the visions returned, growing worse with every passing night. She woke in the morning feeling haggard and looking worse. Myrta had always been more comely than she, but soon the innkeeper kept Rose confined to the kitchen while Myrta was sent to serve the patrons. As a result, Myrta brought considerably more coins to their small stash, and on top of the growing agony from the visons was the humiliating knowledge that she'd never survive without Myrta. It was only Myrta's hard work and devotion that kept any hope alive.

But she couldn't make the visions stop. They woke her more frequently and she grew more tired and worn the longer she and Myrta stayed in this little village.

Tonight was the worst of all. Tonight, she saw herself order the execution of her family. All of them. Her beautiful, simple mother. Her brothers. Nieces and nephews.

Why? Why would she do such a thing? How could she?

The only answer was the sound of her own half-choked sob.

Beside her, Myrta stirred. She reached out and grasped Rose's hand. "Another nightmare?"

Rose nodded, though she knew Myrta couldn't see her in the dark. "We have to leave. Get further away."

Myrta sighed deeply. "We'll find a way, m'lady. Soon."

Myrta rolled over and went back to sleep, but Rose stayed awake, replaying the vision in her mind, over and over. She could not become that kind of a queen. She would not.

41

She just hoped her family—and the kingdom—understood one day why she'd been forced to do what she did. That things would've been worse, so much worse, if she'd stayed.

Healer

Jyn urged her horse to go faster. Where was Taurin? She was sure his horse had fled this direction, but there was no telling how far he'd gone since then, or whether he'd changed direction.

These rocks looked small from a distance, but they were big enough to hide a man.

Or a body.

The ground was too hard-packed and dry to reveal much of a trail, but Jyn thought she saw part of a hoof mark. She turned her horse and guided it up between the rocks.

There! Was that blood?

It was. A distinct trail, growing more pronounced the further it went.

The blood trail meandered through the rocks and then down toward the lowlands and eventually into the desert.

Nyn's backside, she cursed.

This was not good. At least if he'd been in the rocks, he might've had some shade and protection from scavengers.

Jyn spurred her horse to a trot and followed the blood spatter in to the desert.

It went too long. He couldn't survive that much blood loss, not to mention that many hours baking in the sun.

As if in answer to her thoughts, a circle of buzzards formed in the sky overhead.

"No, no, no!" She would spare him that, at least.

She raced forward. In the distance, a mound on the desert floor began to distinguish itself as more than a shadow. A few more moments and she reined her horse in and jumped from his back.

Taurin's chest moved, ever so slightly. He was alive!

Jyn grabbed her canteen and poured little dribbles of water into Taurin's mouth. Then she tore his shirt away to inspect his wound.

He'd yanked the spear right out, taking chunks of flesh with it and leaving a wide, festering wound that seeped into the cracked ground beneath him.

Overhead, the buzzards called to one another, their cries echoing across the valley.

Jyn tore a strip from her shirt and wound it around Taurin's bleeding shoulder. She tightened it securely and knelt to lift him.

He was heavier than she'd thought. His lean physique had never seemed intimidating, but trying to lift his dead weight took more effort than she'd imagined. She crouched to a squat and pulled him by his good arm up over her shoulder, then held on to her horse's saddle for leverage as she stood. Her horse seemed to understand her urgency and stood still as she heaved Taurin's body over the saddle.

Jyn whistled, hoping Taurin's horse was still nearby, but it didn't appear and she didn't have time to look for it. It might already be too late. She mounted the horse and wedged herself behind and slightly under Taurin, then urged her horse toward the road that led back to Nynthavin.

Normally, she'd treat field wounds herself. She had enough experience to do a tolerable job with healing, but if Taurin could be saved, it would take more skill than she had. She had to go to the one place she was least welcome. The palace from where the soldiers who had vomited from the caravan originated. The royal palace where she'd only just days before left her brother under the watchful eyes of the king of Sunnland's royal guard.

The sun moved too quickly in its path along the sky. Her horse moved too slowly. Nynthavin was too far away. She urged the horse along, promising him water and oats if he would only hurry. The gates to the city would stay open for another hour or so, until sundown. Jyn urged the horse to his limits. If they were locked out in the dusty plains overnight, they'd both be dead.

The sun sank lower in the sky, and Jyn's horse was nearly depleted of energy when the city walls came into sight. Jyn pressed on, and they arrived just as the first warning bells tolled.

The horse seemed to sense that the end was near and managed to find another well of energy.

The palace was situated at the center of the city, surrounded by a second wall. Built into the wall were a series of small homes. Servants of the king who were required to be nearby in case they were needed, but were not important enough to receive an apartment within the castle proper. It was to one of these that Jyn fled.

She leapt from the back of the horse and pounded on the door.

"Who is it?" a gruff voice called out.

"It's Jyn. Please, it's an emergency." She pounded again.

A moment later, the door was opened by a sultry maid wearing a blanket.

Jyn looked past her to where Gorym emerged from his bedchamber, tucking his shirt into his trousers.

"I need help. Quickly." Jyn didn't wait for him to respond before turning around and going back to Taurin.

"Nyn's backside, Jyn, what happened?" Gorym demanded as he joined her.

She knew he didn't really expect an answer, though. At least not out here. Without another word, he hoisted Taurin onto his shoulders, carried him inside, and set him on the high table behind a curtain on the far side of the room.

Gorym's lady friend apparently had the sense to put some clothes on. She emerged wearing a simple dress and looking embarrassed.

Gorym pressed a silver bantar into her hand and kissed her cheek. "Go to the temple and offer a prayer to Nyn for healing for the king's faithful soldier."

The girl left, closing the door behind her, and Gorym turned immediately to Taurin. He ripped away the makeshift bandage Jyn had wrapped around Taurin's shoulder. He sucked in his breath and shook his head in a manner that did not inspire much confidence.

"Is he alive?" Jyn asked.

Gorym nodded. "Barely. It's good you brought him as soon as you did. Hand me that bottle, the big blue one on the end."

Jyn turned to his apothecary shelves behind her and located the bottle. Gorym poured the liquid liberally into the wound. He cleaned the

46

hole with a fresh cloth and the liquid from the bottle, carefully digging out bits of splinters from the spear and dirt from the desert.

"This doesn't look good, Jyn," he muttered. "I can sew it closed, but the chance of infection is huge with a wound like this one. Even if he survives the infection, he might never get the use of this arm back. Not to mention the amount of blood he's lost."

Tears stung Jyn's eyes. "Please, Gorym. Isn't there anything else you can do?"

"I wish I could, but I'm already being watched on suspicion of sorcery. They confiscated most of my herbs. Anything that even looked like it might have magical properties."

A tear rolled down Jyn's cheek. "I can't lose him."

Gorym took a deep breath. "Hold on." He disappeared into his bedchamber and returned a moment later with a small amulet and a leather pouch. From the pouch, he took a pinch of powder and mixed it with something from another vial on his shelves and rubbed it on the amulet. He then put the amulet against Taurin's wound and muttered something unintelligible.

"That's the best I can do." He hid the pouch and the amulet back in his bedchamber and began stitching closed Taurin's wound.

Just as he was finishing, the door burst open and the king's soldiers flooded into the room.

"Well, well. What do we have here?" the one at the front, a man wearing general's stripes, asked.

Jyn pulled a knife and flung it at the general. He dodged just at the last moment and the knife sank into the arm of the soldier behind him.

Gorym sank to his knees. "Please, General, I had no choice. She forced me to help her."

Jyn gritted her teeth, but she couldn't blame him. Being caught helping an outlaw would lead to consequences she couldn't ask him to face.

The general eyed her. "We've been looking for you for a long time. You're lucky the king wants you alive."

Jyn blinked. The king wanted her? Alive?

That could not be good. She glanced at Taurin, still lying nearly lifeless on the table.

"Don't worry. If you behave, you'll see him again. Assuming this one knows what he's doing. Come on, then. With me."

47

Jyn glanced at Gorym. He nodded, ever so slightly. Not that it mattered. She didn't have much choice. She squared her shoulders and nodded to the general. "Take me to the king."

Spy

Jyn knelt before the magistrate, her head bowed submissively. Nyn's backside, she hated being made to feel so small.

More, she hated leaving Taurin alone so long.

What happened after she was taken? Had Gorym been arrested, too? Would Taurin be well enough to stay out of sight? And what had the guard meant when he said the king wanted her alive? Had her brother done something stupid while she was away? She'd promised to get him out, why couldn't he trust her?

At last, the bailiff nudged her with his boot, indicating it was her turn.

She tensed, waiting for the magistrate to address her from his dais.

"Well, well. Jyn the Pirate. We've been looking for you for a long time. It was thoughtful of you to bring your activities inland."

"I am sorry, m'lord, but I know not what you speak. I am a simple trader." She dared a look through her lashes at the magistrate.

He nodded at the bailiff, who grabbed her arm and yanked up her sleeve.

The brand marking her as a victim of the king's justice, though no longer red and tender, was still clearly visible.

"Please, m'lord, that was many years ago. I am an honest citizen."

"Then why did the king's guards see you with a band of thieves only this morning?"

Jyn's heart sank. "Can you be sure it was me? I was nowhere near any bandits. I was at the market this morning."

"I see. So this isn't yours, then?"

Jyn looked up. From his finger dangled a gold chain on which hung a large pearl, set in a delicate housing of fine gold shaped like an open oyster shell.

The necklace Taurin had given her, to remind her of the sea, the day she'd agreed to join his band on land. "Where did you find that?"

"One of the king's soldiers took it from one of the bandits who attacked the caravan this morning."

"That's not true. I wasn't wearing it... today. Someone must've stolen it from my home while was... at the market."

"The king's guard swears it was taken from a bandit."

"It's a lie!"

"You expect me to believe the word of a known pirate over one of the king's own men?"

Someone was setting her up. Someone who knew how much the necklace meant to her—knew she'd never deny her ownership of it. But who? And why? "Perhaps the bandit stole it from me before he attacked the caravan?" Jyn suggested.

The disdainful laugh the magistrate directed her way filled the room.

It sounded implausible to her, too, but she had no way to prove she was being framed. Especially since she *had* robbed the caravan earlier.

"Jyn the Pirate, I declare you guilty of banditry. I hereby sentence you to ten years in the restitution prison, after which your thieving hand will be removed."

Jyn choked. *Ten years?* Few people survived five, working to repay their debt to the kingdom in the slave fields and mills. Even if she did survive, when her time was up, they'd cut off her hand, ensuring she'd never be fit for anything but begging.

The magistrate raised his hand, signaling his sentence was final.

Jyn didn't even have time to protest, to beg for mercy, before the bailiff grabbed her arms and yanked them behind her back.

She opened her mouth, but cut off as the door to the court slammed open and King Wyllym himself marched in.

51

By his side was a face she recognized only too well.

"Stoke," she breathed. What was her brother doing here? With the king?

"Bring the prisoner to my conference room immediately," the king said.

The bailiff roughly shoved Jyn toward the door, following the king and Stoke up through the bowels of the castle to the ornately decorated halls above, and finally to a small room off the main hallway, near the throne room.

"You may wait outside," the king told the bailiff.

The bailiff looked unsure about leaving the king with a hardened criminal such as herself, but he bowed and retreated.

Jyn looked at Stoke.

The horrible truth hit her like a punch to her gut. "You did this. You set me up."

"Dearest sister, whatever do you mean?"

"You told me you were a prisoner. That you were being watched. I told you the plan so I could help get you out. And you set up an ambush." She glanced at the king from the corner of her eye, then glared at Stoke. "So you bought your position as trusted advisor with my life. How noble of you."

The king cleared his throat.

Jyn dropped to her knees. "My apologies, Your Majesty."

She gulped, trying to think. He hadn't ordered her immediate death. Instead, he'd ordered her brought to his conference room. And the guard said he wanted her alive. That meant there still might be a way to get out of this.

She took a deep breath and raised her head, ever so slightly. "I am your majesty's loyal servant. Everything I did was out of love for my dear brother. I pray that I may be forgiven and that I may prove myself to you, my king. How may I be of service?"

Stoke coughed, a sound she knew to mean he wasn't buying her words, but the king spoke. "I have need of your skills."

"I am yours to command, my king."

"There are rumors of an alliance being formed between Cadalania and Kirland. They hope to overthrow me and divide my kingdom between them. I am told you possess a certain flair for ferreting information. I need you to discover whether the rumors are true, and if so, devise a way to subvert their plans. In exchange, your sentence will be commuted."

"You wish me to be a spy."

"Spy is such a harsh word," Stoke smiled. "But yes. Or, you can be a slave and finish out your sentence in the fields."

Jyn dared a glance at the king. "Why me?"

King Wyllym chuckled. "Your brother assures me you're the best."

Jyn snorted. "Twenty-five years of hardly noticing me, and now is when you choose to appreciate my skills? Very well, your Majesty. As it happens, my brother is not wrong in this matter. I gladly swear to you my fealty and pledge myself your faithful spy."

The City

Rose brushed a strand of sweat-soaked hair from her face.

Myrta brushed past her, carrying a tray of tankards. "You'd best get back in the kitchen. If Mistress sees you resting, she'll take a piece of your hide."

Rose nodded and hurried back to the kitchen. She'd never worked so hard in her life. Her once-soft hands were callused and dry, her elegant fingernails chipped and dirty. Her gold hair hung in greasy strands rather than soft, clean waves. Fine clothes and jewels had done much to disguise her plain features, but now, wearing a plain dress and covered in grime, she was acutely aware of how homely she really was. Myrta, with her full bosom and dimpled smile, drew eyes and coins from patrons in the common room, while Rose was relegated to the basin to wash dishes more often than not.

Mistress Lambkin bustled into the kitchen.

Rose straightened quickly and thrust her hands into the dishwater.

"The rain is bringing folks in by droves. Hurry up there, we need clean cups and bowls."

"Yes, Mistress," Rose mumbled. She scrubbed the dishes more vigorously.

Over a month since she and Myrta had begged for employment at the inn, and still Rose's father's soldiers hadn't caught up. Or, perhaps they'd passed this little town entirely. At any rate, Rose knew she couldn't stay here much longer. Though she'd learned to work hard, the sleepless, nightmare-ridden nights and long, wearying days grew harder to endure. It was high time she and Myrta moved on from this place.

That night, after the patrons had drunk their last and meandered home, and she and Myrta lay on their hard pallet in the back store room, Rose rolled over to face Myrta.

"We should continue our journey soon. It seems as though my father's soldiers aren't coming for us. We've saved enough wages to get us to the city where there will be more opportunity for both of us."

Washing dishes and being spat upon by drunks was not the adventure she'd pictured when she left home. She'd only left to save her kingdom, and if she thought she'd succeeded she could have endured, but her dreams told her Legerdemain was still in danger, so staying in near slavery seemed pointless.

"Very well, m'lady. I suggest we wait until after the holy day, two weeks hence. We're likely to make more money, as people are more generous when they believe their goddess is watching, and we can use that time to prepare. I expect we'll need a clearer picture of where we're going before we set off again into unknown territory."

Rose nodded. "You're right, of course. I will be patient, but I confess, I'm eager to leave this place."

Having a plan gave Rose new energy, and she spent the next week smiling harder on the occasions when she served the patrons who came to the inn and collecting more coins for her trouble. She tucked away every coin she didn't spend on food, stashing it until she and Myrta had what seemed to be a small fortune.

The day after the holy day, the citizens of the little town slept late, their libations of the night before still lingering, but Myrta had found a tradesman who planned on leaving early for the city. For a price—more than Myrta said it was worth—he agreed to let the two of them ride in his wagon.

Rose noted the slight scowl wrinkling Myrta's brow as she counted out the coins.

"I know it's a lot, but it's better than walking that far. We'd spend that much in food because it would take us three times as long," Rose said.

Myrta smiled at her. "Of course." She climbed into the wagon and reached down to help Rose up.

The countryside grew more lush with every passing mile, and the villages grew closer together. The heat, too, increased, until sweat beaded on Rose's forehead even sitting in the shade of the wagon. The air took on a heavy feel and a strange, tangy scent filled Rose's nose.

They spent the night in the barn of a village inn not unlike the one they'd just left, while the merchant stayed inside, and left before the sun was up the next morning.

"Comin' out of the high country," the merchant said around mid-morning. "Smell that sea air? Won't be long, now."

Rose inhaled deeply, her sense of adventure returning.

The city. She'd never seen one. The Four Villages in Legerdemain were only slightly larger than the village where she and Myrta had spent the last couple months, and the nearness of their destination filled her with a renewed excitement. She reached out and grabbed Myrta's hand.

"We're almost there. Our new lives—our real lives—are about to begin."

Myrta smiled and squeezed back.

By late afternoon, the road had widened and carts and wagons bounced along, narrowly missing one another as they hurried to and from the city.

At long last, the city gates came into view. Rose stared in awe. More than twice as high as the wall that surrounded her palace, the wall that surrounded Nynthavin seemed impenetrable.

A huge archway opened the city up to the road they traveled. Huge, iron gates hung from massive stone pillars. They were open now, but when closed they'd be nearly impossible to break through. The merchant rolled through the archway, his horses seeming to know the end of their journey was near and picking up their pace.

They rode to a long, open area lined with tents and shops. The merchant stopped in front of one tent with the sides battened down, opened one end, and started unloading his cart. "Come morning, when the market opens, you'll not be able to walk through here for all the folks coming and going," he said. "You two'll want to get shelter for the night. You won't want to be caught out after curfew."

"Curfew?" Rose asked.

He nodded. "Patrols start after the ten bell. Anyone out after that is a criminal."

He ignored them, then, as he finished unloading his cart into his little shop tent.

"Where should we go?" Rose asked.

Myrta took her hand. "I saw some inns back near the city gate. We'll go there."

They trudged back the way they had come as darkness blanketed the city. From somewhere in the center of the city a bell chimed.

Rose counted nine. "How long until the tenth?"

"I don't know," Myrta said, her steps quickening.

At last, they reached the hospitality district, an area lined with inns.

Myrta opened the door of a cozy, pleasant looking building and asked the innkeeper how much for a room for the night.

Rose didn't understand the currency in this city, but Myrta's face went white.

"What?"

"One night will cost us nearly all we have," Myrta said.

"That can't be. We've saved for weeks," Rose said.

"Do you have serving that needs to be done or dishes to be washed?" Myrta asked the innkeeper.

"We don't take no beggars," the innkeeper snarled. "Try the Thorn and Pony." He nodded toward the end of the street.

Myrta led the way to the inn he indicated, a dilapidated affair that smelled of urine and vomit.

"We can't stay here," Rose said.

The bell started to chime again.

"We don't have a choice," Myrta said. She pushed open the door and asked the innkeeper about working for a room.

He nodded. "Go 'round back. Shyrin will set you up."

Myrta and Rose followed his grubby, pointed finger around the outside of the inn to a stinking alleyway. Rats crisscrossed in front of them, scurrying over piles of refuse. Rose choked back the bile that threatened to spew out of her.

Ahead, by the back door, someone was talking.

"Please, Shyrin, you know I'm good for the money. I just need to borrow one of your girls for the night," a man said.

Rose shuddered. This place got worse by the minute.

"It's market tomorrow. You know how busy we are. I can't send my girls running off to tend to your needs. What happened to Jyn?"

"I don't know, that's what I'm trying to tell you."

"Can't. You're on your own. And you'd best hurry. Ten bell is chiming."

57

The man groaned and clutched his shoulder. His knees sagged.

In the dim light, Rose saw blood seep from under the man's hand.

Heedless of the filth, she rushed forward. "You're hurt."

The man looked at her through fever-glazed eyes. "You could tell that, could you?"

"Let me take a look."

Myrta pulled on her hand. "We have to get inside." She turned to Shyrin who still stood in the doorway. "The innkeeper said we could work for a room."

"C'mon in. I can always use a pretty face for servin'," Shyrin said, though she wasn't looking at Myrta's face.

"You need a room?" the injured man said. "I have a house not far from here. You can stay with me."

Rose eyed him. "How much?"

"No money. Just some cooking and helping me. I can barely move."

"No," Myrta said. "We don't know him. He could be a brigand for all we know."

"Oh, he's a brigand. Of the worst sort," Shyrin said.

"That I am. But my house is clean and I have food. I just need…" he groaned again and leaned against the wall. "I just need…"

Rose looked from the injured man to the grimy inn. She tucked her shoulders under the man's good arm for support. "Which way?"

The man indicated the other side of the alley.

Myrta stood for a moment, as though deciding what to do, then hurried after Rose and the injured man.

Rose smiled.

Myrta didn't, but her voice held a note of tenderness when she said, "Well, someone has to keep you safe from your own foolishness."

A Place to Stay

Rose helped the bleeding man to the small cot in his upper-story dwelling. It was one of many rooms that comprised the three-level building of living spaces. It was dingy and bare, decorated sparsely with rickety furniture and a few dishes, but clean, as promised.

The man groaned and lost consciousness.

Rose found a bowl on a shelf and handed it to Myrta. "Go get some water. There was a fountain in the courtyard. Hurry."

Myrta scurried to obey and Rose pulled the tattered shirt off the man. A wound in his shoulder seeped blood and pus. Someone had treated it and stitched it closed, but it had been days, at least.

"What happened to you?" she murmured.

She scoured the shelves for any sign of herbs or food, but other than a bit of crusty bread, there was nothing. She waited anxiously until Myrta returned with the water. She found a rag and used it to carefully clean away the blood from around the wound.

A slight greenish tint glowed along the veins surrounding the wound. Someone had used magic to try to heal him. But magic was illegal in Sunnland. Who would dare risk it, especially for a man who, by all appearances, was poor and without standing?

The magic was good, though. If she could draw on that, she might be able to refresh the spell that was used and help him heal. Of course, there were no herbs or anything with remotely magical properties in this little dwelling. Perhaps she could buy some.

In the meantime, she cleaned the wound as well as she could and used a clean rag to bind it again.

"Myrta, we need food, and so does he. Go to the inn and see if you can buy us some soup and bread."

Myrta clutched the tiny purse of their scant coins. Her jaw hardened, but she nodded. "Yes, m'lady."

Rose winced. It had been weeks since Myrta had called her "m'lady" instead of "Rose," and the return to formality hinted at Myrta's displeasure. But she couldn't worry about that now. Myrta would see this was by far the preferable option.

The tiny cot was the only place to sleep in the room, and she couldn't really move the invalid from it, so Rose spread her and Myrta's cloaks on the floor. She found a pot and filled it with water from the fountain, then hung it from the hook in the small fireplace in the corner of the room. She'd never seen anything quite like the fireplace. It was hollow at the back, the chimney running both up and down, apparently sharing the same chimney with the apartments beneath it. Probably the same stones were used for the chimney in the next room over, as well, so four dwelling spaces on each level could use the same chimney.

It was a smart design, allowing the landlord to have several more tenants in each building for a lower cost than in the rows of one-level homes that each had their own fireplace, like in the North Village in Legerdemain where the miners lived. Perhaps when she went back…

No, she had to stop thinking like that. She was never going back.

"Jyn."

Rose looked up. The man stirred, blinking.

"Jyn?"

Rose hurried to his side. "No, I'm Rose. I don't know Jyn."

"She'll come. When she can. Who are you?"

"I met you outside a tavern. You said my friend and I could stay here if we helped you."

"Right. Thank you. How bad is it?"

"Pretty bad. It's infected. Do you know if someone used magic on you?"

He nodded.

"Traces of the spell are still there. I can revive it, but I'll need ingredients."

"No. If you get caught you'll be executed."

61

"I know. But if I don't, the infection will take over and you'll die. Where do I get herbs and things?"

"There's a market in the center of town. I'm not sure you'll find what you're looking for, though. There are strict laws against selling magical plants."

Rose shook her head. "Magic is nature. All things that are connected to the earth have innate magical properties, which is why herbs and certain gems are particularly potent, but I can draw magical elements from anything green."

"How do you know these things?"

"There was a woman who lived in my father's ca…village. She taught me many of her arts."

The man nodded. "The market will be open during the day. I'll take you tomorrow. "

"You're in no shape to go anywhere. Myrta and I will go, if you'll tell us where."

"I'm not sending you into the market alone. If I make it through the night, I'll be well enough to go."

Rose crossed her arms, prepared to protest, but before she had a chance to argue, Myrta returned bearing a tureen of fragrant soup and a loaf a bread.

"Thank you, Myrta," Rose said. She turned to the man. "Can you eat?"

He nodded and struggled to sit up. "Where did you get that?"

"The inn," Myrta said. Her voice held a note of bitterness. "You claimed you had food, but there's nothing in this place."

The man's chuckle quickly turned to a groan, as though laughing caused his injury more pain. "I wasn't lying." He pushed himself up from the cot, despite Rose's protests, and made his way to the shelf where the sparse dishes where lined up. He moved the bowls from the top shelf and opened a hidden cupboard in the wall. From it, he pulled dried meat, tea, butter, and dried fruit.

More rich food than Rose and Myrta had eaten in months. A feast fit for a king. Or at least a wealthy merchant.

Beneath the food was another hidden compartment, from which the man pulled a small bag of coins. He handed it to Myrta. "To repay you for what you spent, with my eternal thanks."

Rose stared at him. "Who *are* you?"

The door burst open, cutting off whatever response he would have given. A woman with short, curly brown hair, dressed in trousers, stomped in.

Her shoulders relaxed and her face softened when she saw the man. "Taurin. You're alive."

So he had a name. Taurin. Rose liked it. Srong, noble. It suited him.

Taurin nodded. "Thanks to these ladies."

The woman turned, seeming to notice Rose and Myrta for the first time. Her eyes raked over them briefly before she turned back to Taurin. "I can't stay. I said I had to retrieve something from home, but if I don't come back, they'll hunt me down. I just had to make sure you hadn't been captured, too."

"Captured?" Taurin said. "What do you mean?"

The woman shook her head. "I'm fine. I just have to do a job, and then I'll be free. I'll meet up with you soon. Be safe."

She disappeared through the door, slamming it behind her.

Rose stared after her for a long moment before looking back at Taurin. What had she gotten herself into?

Outlaws

Taurin stretched. The girl, Rose, knew her healing arts. He felt better than he had before the injury. He watched her in the corner, trying desperately to match the motions of her friend as they built a fire and prepared dinner, but she clearly was unaccustomed to such work.

She'd been nobility, of that he was certain, except that made no sense, because she claimed to be from Zyan, a land without distinctions between classes. Kirland seemed more likely, except that she knew magic, and Kirland was almost as strict as Sunnland when it came to regulating magic use. Where she was from, who she really was, remained as much a mystery now as it had been two weeks ago when they met.

She must've felt Taurin's eyes on her, for she turned toward him and smiled. Rose wasn't particularly beautiful—her friend was by far the prettier of the two—but that smile was blessed by Nyn herself.

Rose ladled a bowl of soup and came to sit beside him. She handed him the bowl. "I'm afraid it's the best we can do until we can afford to buy more supplies."

Taurin smiled and took a bite. "It's wonderful."

"Speaking of…" Rose twisted her hands in her lap. "I fear we have taken advantage of your hospitality long enough. Your wound is nearly healed, and we… we ought to be moving on soon."

"Moving on to where?"

Rose shrugged. "I don't know, exactly. We just need to get far away from… here. Settled somewhere safe. And I would hate to put you in danger on our behalf."

Taurin raised an eyebrow. "Danger? You mean because you can use magic?"

On the other side of the room, Myrta coughed conspicuously.

Rose glanced at her, then looked back at her hands. "Yes. Because of that. I understand it's outlawed here."

Taurin nodded. "It is."

"We were thinking of going west. Across the sea," Rose went on. "Maybe all the way to the Silver Shores."

"The trip across the sea is treacherous. If you can even find passage, it will be expensive. How will you pay for it?"

Rose shrugged. "I suppose we'll have to work to save enough."

"And where will you live in the meantime? In the city?"

Tears threatened to spill from her blue eyes, but she set her chin and said, "We'll figure something out."

Taurin frowned. Jyn would tell him these waifs were not his responsibility, that they couldn't be trusted, that he'd be better off letting them leave. But something in the way Rose bravely made her decisions, the way she tried hard to learn skills that were clearly new to her, the way she risked herself to help him—she was intriguing, to say the least. And the gentle touch of her hands as she worked to heal his wounds endeared her all the more.

He wasn't quite ready for her to disappear forever. "Have you considered going east?" he asked.

Myrta's head snapped up and she gave Taurin a look that seemed to be a mixture of caution and anger.

"East?" Rose asked. "You mean to the desert?"

Taurin shook his head. "The mountains."

"The mountains are nothing but jagged, uninhabitable rocks. At least, that's what I've always heard."

"For the most part, that's true. But there are valleys, accessible only through nearly impassable trails, beyond the regularly patrolled routes, where people can live. I know of one such place where there lives a group of people who are… shall we say… in no hurry to risk showing their faces in view of the king's men."

Rose scrunched her eyebrows together. "I don't understand."

Taurin took a deep breath. How could a member of nobility be so adorably naïve?

Before he could reply, Myrta said in a tone dripping with disdain, "They're outlaws, Rose. People who have escaped the king's justice and are living in hiding."

Rose turned her innocent gaze on Taurin. "Is that true?"

Taurin wouldn't lie to her. "Yes. And some of them are violent criminals. But most of them just want to live in peace and carry on with their lives."

Rose tilted her head slightly. "But what would we do? Myrta can do anything she sets her mind to, but I… my skills are of a specific sort that are not terribly useful amongst a group of outlaws."

Taurin smiled. "We don't have a Healer in the group, and as this," he tapped his wounded shoulder, "has made clear, we desperately need one. And you wouldn't have to worry about hiding your ability to use magic. You'd be welcome just as you are."

"You said 'we.' Are you… are you an outlaw, too, then?"

Taurin grinned. "Aye, madam. A bandit, to be precise. I keep this apartment to sleep in when I come to town to sell my wares, but my home is in the mountains."

"And your friend, the angry one?"

Taurin chuckled. He could well see why she described Jyn that way. "Jyn is a pirate."

Rose nodded. "I see. Myrta and I will have to discuss it, but we will let you know our answer soon."

"I'll be ready to leave in two days. You're welcome to stay with me until then, either way."

Rose smiled. "Thank you."

Taurin handed her the empty soup bowl and rolled over on his small cot, feigning sleep.

The women worked quietly for a while. Just as Taurin thought he might actually fall asleep, Rose whispered, "I think we should go with him."

"Are you mad?" Myrta hissed. "You want to live in a colony of thieves and murderers and who can say what other kinds of brigands?"

"They'll never look for us there," Rose insisted.

"And you still insist we mustn't go back?"

Rose's sigh filled the small apartment. "I can't."

"The nigthmares."

"They're not just nightmares. It's what I Saw."

"Even after all this, will you not trust me with your thoughts?" Myrta's voice, though low, held a plaintive quality, almost begging, something he'd never expected to hear from a woman as aloof as she.

"I can't," Rose said. "You must trust me on this."

"And when will you trust me, Rose? Trust that I understand people and the world, and that I know what I'm saying when I say this is a very bad plan."

"I do trust you, Myrta. With my life. But that doesn't mean I don't disagree with you. Taurin is a good man. An honest one, despite how he makes his living. We'll be safe with him."

"But m'lady, is this the life you want? Hidden away in the mountains as a common outlaw?"

M'lady. So Taurin had been right. Rose was nobility.

"I *am* common," Rose said. "At least as far as anyone here is concerned. Except that I have no skills that will serve me in this life. Diplomacy by a peasant is hardly a marketable skill, and I doubt the king is looking for help running the country. And magic is outlawed."

"We could follow our original plan and go across the sea."

"When? We have no money, and I won't be dependent on you to earn money to support us and pay our passage."

"You know I'd gladly do that and more for you, m'lady." Myrta sounded hurt.

"I know, Myrta. You've been a dearer friend than I could've imagined, and far better than I deserve. Which is exactly why I cannot continue to take advantage of you. We're equals now, and I must be able to earn my way. Let's go to the mountains, just for a while, and save up our money there until we can afford to move on. Across the sea, as you said."

"Very well, m'lady. As you say." Myrta sounded resigned, though clearly still not pleased at the prospect.

A small thrill ran through Taurin at the thought of having Rose nearby for a bit longer. He'd begin in the morning preparing for his return to the mountains with his two new recruits in tow.

The Camp

The heat from the lowlands didn't dissipate until they were far up into the mountains. Rose wiped sweat from her brow with a cloth Myrta handed her. The cart they sat in jostled over the bumpy trail.

Myrta still seemed uncomfortable with the idea of living in an outlaw camp, but she'd come along anyway.

As they trudged their way up the pass into the mountains, the vegetation thinned and the landscape became more barren. Plants and trees became smaller and more like bushes. Late in the afternoon, Taurin turned the horse off the main path and onto a track that seemed scarcely more than a game trail that rose up a sharp incline, higher into the mountains.

"I apologize, ladies, but I'm going to have to ask you to walk for a bit," Taurin said. "The horse will have enough trouble carrying the supplies up this part." He jumped from his perch at the front of the cart and took the horse's reins to lead him instead of driving him.

Rose jumped down from the back of the cart and hurried up to walk near Taurin. Myrta followed more slowly, and when Rose glanced back, Myrta's eyes proclaiming how much she didn't appreciate Taurin's request.

For more than an hour they hiked up the steep trail, weaving in and out of boulders and zigzagging up the side of the hill. Just when Rose thought she couldn't take another step, Taurin took her hand. "We're almost there. Just around that bend up ahead."

Rose took a swig from the water skin he handed her, then passed it on to Myrta.

Taurin didn't release her hand as he began walking again.

The bend was a narrow space between two rocks, scarcely large enough for the cart to fit through. When they reached it, Taurin let out a series of low whistles that sounded like bird calls.

An answering whistle echoed from beyond the rocks, and Taurin smiled. "They know not to kill you for intruding."

Rose giggled, but Myrta stopped short.

"That was a possibility?" Myrta asked.

"Of course. You don't think we leave our camp unguarded, do you?"

"No trust among thieves?"

"Oh, we trust each other. Just not anyone else. As long as you follow the rules of the camp, you'll be fine."

A spike of panic shot through Rose. "How will we know the rules?"

"The rules are simple. Mind your own business. Don't interfere with anyone else. Don't harm anyone else within the camp, either physically or by harming or stealing their possessions."

"That seems easy enough to live by." Rose smiled.

"Who enforces the rules?" Myrta asked. "What happens if we don't obey them?"

"The rules are enforced by all of us. If someone commits a crime, there must be sufficient evidence for a majority to agree. And if they do agree, then that person is hanged."

Rose gulped.

Myrta nodded, as though such punishment made perfect sense to her, the first sign she'd given that remotely resembled acceptance of their course.

Before Rose could inquire further, they emerged from the narrow pass and came out on an outcropping overlooking a valley. The camp was more like a small village. Trees surrounded it on every side, tall but sparser and less vibrant than the forest that surrounded Legerdemain. The light from the sun setting behind them bathed everything in a soft, golden glow.

The setting reminded her so much of her tiny kingdom. Tears caught in her throat. She would never see home again. But perhaps this quaint, remote community could come to feel like a home to her and Myrta.

"This way," Taurin said. He led them down the narrow path and into the village. Men and women and even a few children came out of little huts to greet him.

One man, several inches taller and broader than Taurin, stepped in their path and crossed his arms over his chest. One of the last rays of sun filtering through the trees on the mountaintop glinted off his shiny bald head. "What do we have here?"

Taurin grinned up at him. "I have good news. I have brought us a Healer."

A gasp rose up around the small crowd gathered, which quickly turned into a clamoring.

Taurin held up a hand. "Patience. We've been traveling all day. Let the Healer and her assistant get settled and she will see patients in the morning." He turned to the big, bald man. "Quentyn, are you willing to lease the cabin by the stream?"

The big man nodded. "Two kadar a month."

Rose blanched. She was still only slightly familiar with the Sunnland money, but that seemed like a preposterous amount.

But Taurin didn't seem to think so. He nodded and handed the big bald man one large gold coin from his pouch. "She'll pay you the rest for this month after she sees some patients."

The big man, Quentyn, grunted, but didn't object.

"Come on." Taurin took Rose's hand again and led and Myrta through the village to the other end, then down a narrow path that wound through the trees to a small cabin. As he'd mentioned, a stream babbled only a few paces away.

That would be good. Rose would need ready access to fresh water for healing.

The cabin was furnished, though sparsely. It had two rooms. A front room contained a fireplace, a table and two chairs, a shelf with some dishes and pots, and some other odds and ends. The back room held two narrow cots, a basin for bathing, and a shelf for clothes.

Rose looked around and breathed deeply. "This will do nicely."

"I'll help you get settled, then," Taurin said. He left to go retrieve the box of herbs Rose had brought from the market in the city.

"I don't trust this place, Rose," Myrta said as soon as he was out of hearing. "These people—criminals. This place—too far away from civilization. This house—who knows who lived here before, or when that man will decide to charge us more than the exorbitant amount he's already charging."

Rose took her hand. "Isn't far from civilization exactly what we were looking for? We'll never be found here. We'll be safe. And we can be happy."

Rose spun in a slow circle. "Magic is rich here. I can feel it in the air, in the rocks and trees. I could become an incredibly powerful Healer in this place. And these people need that. There are children here. They're just trying to make a life for themselves, and we can be part of that."

"That's all well and good for you, but what about me? I'm not your assistant, I'm your servant. I don't know the first thing about Healing."

Rose grinned. "That's the beauty of it. You can be anything you want to be here. Look at this place. There's room for both of us. If I hang a curtain in the main room and get another cot and a shelf for my supplies, I can keep my healing contained to that area, and you can start a business of your own in the other half. We won't need for much, so we won't need money except to pay our rent. I can gather my own herbs and we can plant a garden in the back. We have everything we need here, enough that you can stop worrying about taking care of me and start making yourself into who you want to be."

Schemes

Jyn grimaced as the serving girl pulled tight the laces on her corset.

"Almost done, m'lady," the girl murmured.

For the thousandth time, Jyn thanked Nyn she hadn't been born a noble. She much preferred her trousers and loose-fitting blouses to these torture devices. But she had no choice. As careful as she'd been, one of the king's spies had followed her back to Taurin's apartment. She'd been informed that a guard was posted to watch all his comings and goings, and if she so much as considered running away and not fulfilling her duty to the king, Taurin would be captured and sold at the slave auction.

The servant finished with the laces and slipped a scarlet silk dress over Jyn's head. The gown brushed against Jyn's skin, snug through the bodice and waist, showing every curve, then flaring out from the waist down, full and sweeping. The servant adjusted the ruffles and stepped back. "Very good, m'lady. Now, what to do with your hair."

She examined the dark curls which Jyn kept cut short. "This is good. It looks exotic." She smeared grease into Jyn's hair, twisting the curls and securing them with tiny gems. When she finished, she applied thick layers of cosmetics to Jyn's face. "Perfect," she said at last. "The king will be well pleased. Have a look."

She led Jyn to the tall looking glass that stood against one wall.

Jyn gasped. She barely recognized herself. The dark lines around her eyes made them appear narrow and sultry against the pale powder that covered her face. Her lips stood out, full and red. The way her hair was styled made it appear that her dark ringlets were longer than they really were, and the corset under the form-fitting dress made her look as though she had full breasts.

What she would give to have Taurin see her like this!

A knock at the door pulled her from her thoughts.

The serving girl opened it to admit a liveried footman. "Is the ambassador ready?"

The serving girl curtsied. "She is." She stepped aside to let Jyn pass.

Jyn held her chin high. If there was one thing she knew how to do, it was bluff her way through any situation. She strode into the ballroom where a bevy of nobles and diplomats mingled, drinking fine wine and chatting. She walked toward the king who stood with two men, one older with a graying beard, and one younger, handsome, clean shaven, with long, black hair held in a tail at the base of his neck.

The king saw her and smiled. "Gentlemen, allow me to introduce her highness, Jinna, the princess of the Silver Shores. Her father has sent her to negotiate a trade agreement. Your highness, this is Lord Pridte, ambassador from Cadalania," he indicated the older man, "and Prince Marckis, of Kirland."

Jyn dipped her head. It was supposed to be a curtsy, but she couldn't bend with the corset holding her straight up and down. "I am... pleased of your... acquaintance." She stumbled over the words, as though the language was difficult, the line rehearsed.

"You highness, might I have the honor of a dance?" Lord Pridte asked.

She stared blankly and gave him a half-hearted smile.

Pridte smiled and gestured toward the dance floor.

Jyn allowed her face to relax in understanding and nodded. She took Pridte's extended arm.

"She can't do much negotiation when she can't speak the language," Prince Marckis commented.

"She has an interpreter for our meetings, but she didn't want to be bothered with too much business. Tonight is supposed to be enjoyable."

Jyn smiled. She couldn't fault the king for his shrewdness. He'd understood immediately her tactics.

73

Lord Pridte led her to the dance floor and pulled her into his arms. "My, but you're a pretty thing," he said.

She gave him her blank smile.

"I wonder if it's true about women from the Silver Shores knowing spells to increase pleasure."

She still smiled.

"Maybe I'll come to your chambers tonight and find out."

She blinked, making her eyes as vacant and uncomprehending as she could.

The nobleman's comments grew more crass the more he believed she couldn't understand. If she had to endure much more of his blatant lust, she'd give up her disguise and make certain his lordship was physically incapable of doing any of the things he suggested ever again.

To her great relief, Prince Marckis cut in.

She turned the same vacant smile on him as they danced. He, too, bought the deception, and spoke freely, although his chatter was inane and superficial.

At last, Prince Marckis stopped dancing and released her. "My apologies, your highness, but I must discuss some business." He started toward Lord Pridte.

Jyn smiled and followed.

"Please excuse us, your highness," Lord Pridte said.

Jyn lowered her lashes and gave Prince Marckis her most seductive smile, then turned her gaze on Lord Pridte.

"Oh, what can it hurt?" Pridte said. "She can't understand us anyway, and we'd do well to keep her happy. We might need her later."

Prince Marckis paused, then nodded his agreement. "This way." He led Pridte to a balcony that overlooked the royal gardens.

"King William is shrewd," Prince Marckis began. "He has the finest ports and trade routes, and he knows it."

Jyn walked to the balcony and gazed at the gardens, trying to appear disinterested in the conversation.

"Kirland has ports," Marckis went on, "but so much of our country is marshland, it's hard to access them except from within our own borders."

Pridte grunted. "And Cadalania has industry and crops, but we have to pass through Sunnland to get to Kirland, and William's taxes and fees make that route even less appealing. We need a trade route that will circumvent Sunnland if we are to come to an accord."

"Precisely," Marckis said.

"You have a suggestion?" Pridte's voice sounded eager.

"Legerdemain."

"Legerdemain?" Pridte scoffed. "That country is so small, no one has even bothered to try to take it over in seven hundred years. Their only export is gems, and even those are limited enough that it's not worth the effort to try to take the country."

"That is precisely what makes it so valuable. It is protected to the north by the Soulless Mountains, and on all sides by a great forest and a mighty river that serves as a moat. Any nation would be foolish to waste resources trying to take it. But if an agreement could be reached…"

"Impossible," Pridte said. "Legerdemain never gets involved in politics outside its own borders."

"Indeed. But imagine if we could convince them to let us have access to the river. Cadalanian ships could travel straight to Kirland's ports. We would increase trade between our countries and beyond the sea. Both our nations would prosper."

"That would be brilliant, but why would Legerdemain consider it, after all this time?"

"It would benefit them, as well. It would give them a better route for exporting their gems, and give them access to more imports."

Jyn turned just enough to study Marckis's face. The man was cunning. He had a plan.

"And you think you have a way to convince them?" Pridte asked.

"I'm still working on that," Marckis said. "But if you and I come to an accord, if I have your assurance that Cadalania will be Kirland's ally in any negotiations, I can plan my strategy accordingly."

"You have my pledge. I'll sign and seal it first thing in the morning."

Jyn pretended not to notice when Pridte nodded toward her. "What about her?"

"I'll schedule a meeting with her and her interpreter. I have no doubt that between us we can offer her Highness a trade deal that will far surpass anything Sunnland will be able to negotiate. Come. We should get back before we're missed."

Marckis touched Jyn's arm and she jumped, as though startled, before smiling up at him. She took his arm as he led her back to the ballroom.

As they approached the dance floor, he started to release her arm, so she turned to face him, as though she'd thought he'd intended to dance with her. She held up her arms in the position for the waltz that played.

As she'd anticipated, he couldn't very well leave her standing alone on the dance floor like that. He pulled her close and joined the dance.

Jyn smiled at him. She had to find out what he had planned. He was too savvy to share all his secrets with a tentative ally like Lord Pridte, but a man would share his darkest secrets in bed. Especially if he thought his bedmate would spread no tales. It was why the Pleasure Guild made their prostitutes deaf and mute—they fetched a higher price.

Jyn stepped closer, pressing her body into his, lightly caressing his shoulder where her hand rested with her fingertips. She looked up into his eyes and ran her tongue over her lips. She made the invitation as explicit as she could without uttering a word.

Marckis sighed deeply and held her. "Ah, my dear, I wish I could. But I cannot risk a misunderstanding. It would not do for you to have a claim on me if I am to marry the crown princess of Legerdemain."

The waltz ended and Marckis bowed. "Thank you for the dance, your highness."

He turned and strode away, stopping when he reached a group of nobles and joining their conversation.

That was just as well for Jyn. It took all her powers of control to keep her expression flirtatious and uncomprehending when he'd spilled his plan. She could hardly wait to tell the king. With luck, this news would be enough to set her—and Taurin—free.

Settling In

Rose carefully mixed the herbs in the little pestle, then put them in the bowl and added hot water to make a paste. She dabbed the concoction on Quentyn's wound. "This will help dull the pain so I can put stitches in. It will also help ward off infection and promote healing. You will have a nasty scar, though."

The big man grunted.

"Quentyn doesn't mind that," Taurin said from where he sat stoking the fire. "He thinks women find scars attractive."

Quentyn growled, and Rose and Taurin shared a smile.

Rose stitched the wound closed, covered it with more of the paste, and bandaged it. "All done," she said. "No more chasing kittens under the porch."

"Man's got to do what a man's got to do to keep his woman happy."

Rose smiled. That was the most words she'd ever heard from him.

Quentyn pressed a handful of coins into her palm and stalked out.

Rose stared at the money in her hand. "This is too much. All I did was sew up a cut." She looked at Taurin. "I'll be right back. I must return some."

Taurin jumped up and grabbed her arm.

Rose's heart sped up at the warmth of his fingers on her skin. She looked up into his eyes.

"Don't," he said. "It would be very offensive to him. He paid you for the value he placed in your work, not the time or effort you put in."

Rose pondered that, though her mind kept returning to the feel of Taurin's light touch on her arm. "Like you might give an extra coin to a serving girl for a job well done?"

Taurin nodded. "In a way, yes. But we have our own, unspoken code here. When you first came, Quentyn charged you far more for rent than was fair. I didn't say anything, because I knew you'd have no trouble earning that, for one, and two, because I didn't want anyone to see any sign of weakness in you. Respect must be earned, especially among people who are accustomed to not trusting one another."

Rose understood that. As queen, it would've taken some time for her to gain the people's trust, even though she would've inherited the title rightfully.

"Accepting Quentyn's price was a show of your strength and credibility," Taurin went on. "However, Quentyn cannot lower the price of your rent without looking weak himself, so instead, he finds other ways to compensate, like bringing extra logs for the woodpile and overpaying you for Healing. It's a sign that you have earned his trust and his respect."

Rose smiled. "Thank you for explaining it to me. I want to be accepted here.

Taurin stepped closer, his hand still on her arm, closing the space between them one inch at a time. "Do you? Why is that?"

Rose paused to find her breath, which seemed to have deserted her. "I like it here. It is a place—and a community—I think I could... love. It feels like..." She lifted her face so only a breath of space remained between them. "It feels like home."

"Linens are fresh and clean, Rose." Myrta's voice clanged in through the open door, jarring Rose.

Rose stepped back, her face burning, and began cleaning up her Healing supplies. "Thank you, Myrta."

Myrta paused in the doorway, looking back and forth between Rose and Taurin.

Taurin dusted his hands on his trousers. "I must be going. I'll be at the tavern tonight, if you ladies would care to join me."

"Perhaps," Rose said, at the same time Myrta said, "No, thank you."

79

Taurin smiled at Rose, his gaze warming her to her toes. "I'll see you tonight, then."

Rose barely heard as Myrta told her that the huntress, who supplied the meatseller, had said a laundry service would be a highly profitable business, and a much-needed service to the community.

"That sounds like exactly the sort of thing that would do for you," Rose said, forcing her attention back to her friend. "Of course, you're always welcome to stay with me. The Creator knows I wouldn't have survived without you. I owe you so much."

Myrta smiled. "Thank you, but I need to support myself."

"I know. Your independence and integrity are some of the reasons I admire you so."

Myrta's face flushed.

Rose turned away, so as not to embarrass her friend. Her mind drifted back to Taurin and the way his hands, so strong and capable, could be so gentle. What would they feel like...

She yanked her thoughts back. She had no right to let them wander there.

"Will you come to the tavern tonight?" she asked Myrta.

"No, I'd rather spend a quiet evening," Myrta said. "I'll make dinner, though, if you'd like to stay."

"Thank you, but I think I'll go. I'd like to meet some more of the villagers."

Myrta frowned. "He's not free, you know."

Rose turned to face her. "What do you mean?"

"That woman, the one who came in to check on him that first night. He belongs to her."

Heat infused Rose's cheeks. "He doesn't belong to anyone. Jyn is more like a sister to him. He told me."

"That's not how she feels."

"I can't help how she feels. If it's true, which I don't know, then I regret that she will be disappointed, but I can't help it if he doesn't return her feelings."

Myrta grabbed a bucket for water and stalked out the door. "Don't say I didn't warn you."

A few hours later, Rose pinned her wild curls into place as well as she could and set out. She stood awkwardly at the door of the tavern, peering inside at the people who laughed, drank, and danced in the warm glow of the fire in the hearth and the candles on the walls.

Taurin, sitting at a table with Quentyn and a few others, glanced at the door and saw her. He smiled and jumped up to greet her.

He took her hand and pulled her inside. "Did Myrta come?"

Rose shook her head. "She wanted a quiet evening alone."

"That's a pity. I want her to feel welcome here."

A pang of jealousy shot through Rose. She couldn't blame him. Myrta was beautiful—infinitely more so than Rose. Still, she tried to keep her voice nonchalant. "Oh? Why is that?"

Taurin stopped and faced her. "Because I want you to be happy here. And I know that if Myrta isn't happy, you'll be miserable. You would leave, if she asked you to, just as she was willing to come because you asked her to."

Rose nodded. Myrta had sacrificed so much for her. She wouldn't stay if Myrta insisted on going, no matter how much she loved it.

"I want Myrta to be happy," Taurin went on, his voice low and soft in her ear, "because I want, very deeply, for you to stay."

Rose's face burned. Again. She'd end up looking constantly sunburned if she stayed near him.

His breath tickling her neck convinced her it was worth it. "We shall have to find a way to help her be content, then," she whispered.

They stood there for a long moment before a shout from the table where Taurin had been sitting demanded their attention.

"Come. I must rejoin my band. We're discussing strategy."

"Strategy for what?"

"Not all of us earn our living with an honest trade like Healing. A caravan is due to come through the mountain pass tomorrow, but after what happened last time, we're having to reevaluate how we operate."

"What happened last time?" Rose asked.

Taurin touched his shoulder where she'd Healed the wound that almost killed him. "This happened."

Rose's stomach felt as though it dropped right through the floor. "You're going tomorrow?"

Taurin touched her face with his fingertips. "That's why we're talking. We're going to be careful."

"It's so dangerous."

"That it is. But it's what I do."

Rose's hear thumped in time to the fast-paced jig that someone on the other end of the room fiddled. She had no right to ask him not to go, to suggest he not do as he always had, but the thought of him getting wounded again…

"Rose."

Rose's heart stuttered at the way he said her name. She looked up at him.

"I will come back. But there may be injuries that will need attending when we return. I'll need you to tend to my men. Will you do that for me?"

Rose nodded. She knew, in that moment, that there was nothing she wouldn't do for him.

Trader

"Those are Legerdemain amethysts," Jyn said, holding one of the gems up to the light.

The trader ran a greasy hand through thin, stringy, black hair. "That they are, Madam. The finest in the world. They say that when the last of the dragons died, they hid in caves in the Soulless Mountains to the north, and their bodies became fine gemstones, mined by the Legerdemainians for the last five hundred years, and none are finer than the signature amethyst."

"I'm not interested in old fairy tales. I am, however, interested in why you're selling them at thrice the going rate and trying to pass it off as a bargain."

"Ah, that's where you're mistaken, my dear."

Jyn slid a knife from her sleeve and twirled it in her fingers. "Call me 'my dear' again."

The trader bowed and pulled at his hair. "My apologies, Madam. As I was saying, the supply from Legerdemain is not what it used to be. Some say the mines are drying up. Others say it's because the trade routes are attacked by bandits."

"Bandits have been attacking trade routes since the beginning of time. Why would that make a difference?"

The trader shrugged. "Me, I think it has more to do with political unrest in Legerdemain."

"Oh? How so?"

The trader shrugged again and ran his hands through his hair. "I'm just a simple trader. I don't know much about politics. But sometimes I hear things."

Jyn gave him a conspiratorial smile and leaned forward to make the most of her minimal cleavage. "What did you hear?"

The trader leaned in and whispered. "The king's health is not good and the queen is a simpleton, unable to powder her own nose, let alone run a country. And the heir apparent is..." he paused and looked around the stuffy, shelf-lined tent, as though checking for eavesdroppers. "Missing."

"Missing? What do you mean, missing?"

"The rumor is that she was kidnapped by slave traders."

"That was poor planning, then," Jyn smirked. "Princesses make terrible slaves."

The trader chuckled. "More likely, she was kidnapped for ransom."

"That would make infinitely more sense."

"From what I've gathered, all amethysts are being collected in order to pay the ransom."

Jyn smiled. "Sounds like a pretty shady excuse to drive up prices."

The trader smiled, showing half-rotted teeth. "The price is fair for the market. You'll not find better outside Legerdemain, and possibly not even there."

Jyn grunted her skepticism.

On the other hand, if he was right, she couldn't afford not to get her hands on some before the price went up further. There was no reason she couldn't make a little profit on the side.

Still, she ought to be able to haggle the cost a little bit.

She selected a small handful of the clearest gems in different sizes.

"Twenty-five bantar," the trader said.

Jyn feigned choking. "Twenty-five? The price is going up as we speak, I see."

"I would do three kadar."

Jyn laughed. "How does someone in your line of work survive being so bad at math?"

"Two kadar, five bantar."

"One kadar is more than what these little gems are worth."

Now it was the trader's turn to feign horror. "I'd go out of business in a week if I made deals like that. I can do no less than two."

"I can find a better deal at any other shop." Jyn set the gems back on the table.

"One and eight," the trader said.

"One and five," Jyn countered.

"One and seven."

"Done." Jyn pulled her purse from where it was sewn inside her blouse. She retrieved one large gold coin and seven smaller silver ones and handed them to the trader.

He put her gems in a pouch and tied the drawstrings tightly. "Come back soon."

"At these prices? Ha. You're lucky I was too busy to bother going elsewhere today."

The trader waved as she left the sweltering tent. It was the same dance with every vendor every week, as she invested gold and silver for other goods that she would sell at a profit to the caravan drivers in the city at the monthly bazaar, and words she would sell for her freedom.

Jyn hurried home to her small loft above a stable. The king had allowed her to return home for brief periods—to keep up appearances, he said—so long as she sent daily messages, came in person once a week, and didn't try to slip away from the guards posted to watch her.

She hid the gems and her money in a secret compartment in the wall. Then, she took a tiny roll of parchment and wrote a message.

The lily wilts. The seedling is missing. The lily is ready to be plucked.

She rolled the parchment up and put it in a hollow tube, then took the tube to the roof where her doves waited in their cages. She reached inside and found a particular dove and died the tube to her foot. She stroked the dove's soft feathers. "Be quick, my sweet. The message is urgent."

The dove flew into the air and disappeared, heading for the palace.

Breakfast

Taurin rose early. The room he rented above the bakery, though small, seemed empty and lonely. When Jyn was in the village, she'd stay with him. She didn't have her own place here—she preferred to live in the city—but even if she were there, he'd still have been anxious to leave.

It was another woman's company he sought.

He dressed and trotted down the stairs. The baker, a former enforcer for the king, was a man almost as burly as Quentyn. He'd come to the village after he'd fallen out of favor with the king.

"Good morning, Taurin. Are you off to the Healer's?"

"I am." Taurin chided himself for becoming so predictable, but more out of habit than because he actually cared.

The baker handed him a fresh loaf of bread. "Take this to her, would you? And tell her I said thank you for the herbs. My herb bread is a new favorite at the tavern."

"I'll tell her," Taurin smiled.

He walked down the street. A few men were repairing and extending the boardwalks. Everyone had pitched in money to pay for the materials except those who donated their time and strength to do the actual work.

It wasn't a perfect system—there were always those who shirked responsibility or did the least they could get away with—but pressure from one another and regular meetings to vote on community priorities kept the village functioning as well as any monarchy-run city.

Possibly better.

He stopped by Lili's cottage for eggs. She'd been mistress to some nobleman, until his wife found out, and now she raised chickens and sold eggs and poultry.

Laden with a basket of eggs and bread, Taurin arrived at Rose's cottage. Myrta was already up, lugging buckets of water from the creek to her washtub.

"Good morning, Myrta," Taurin said.

Myrta smiled, but the smile didn't reach her narrowed eyes. She'd gotten more aloof, even as Rose had grown more friendly. While Rose integrated herself into the workings of the village, making friends and sharing ideas and resources, Myrta kept to herself, except to negotiate washing.

"Let me set these down and I'll help you with that," Taurin said. He was determined to make Rose's friend soften toward him.

He set the food on the table and took the two extra buckets that stood by the door down to the creek to fill them. He didn't see Rose, either in the house or down by the creek, but he determined not to ask until he'd helped Myrta.

She ignored him as he carried load after load of water from the creek, filling both her wash basin and her rinse basin. When they were both full, along with the buckets, just in case, Taurin finally asked, "Where is Rose this morning?"

"Gathering herbs."

"Will she be back soon?"

"Don't know."

"Do you know what direction she went?"

Myrta just shrugged.

"Well, then... I'm going to make some eggs."

"You don't have to cook for us," Myrta snapped. "I can handle it."

"I know. But I enjoy cooking, and you're busy. It's no trouble at all."

He slipped inside before Myrta could bark at him again. What would it take to make a friend of that woman?

Rose came home just as he was finishing the eggs. Her cheery voice greeted Myrta, whose surly tones responded softly enough that Taurin couldn't make out what she said.

Rose bounded up the porch stairs and burst into the room, her face alight with a beaming smile. She stood in the doorway for a moment, her figure silhouetted by the morning sun, her breasts heaving with her deep breaths.

Taurin stopped himself from staring and focused on her face. Her cheeks were flushed and pink, dotted by dozens of tiny freckles. Her hair stuck out from around her head in a wild tangle of golden curls. He could imagine how soft her hair would be, curling around his fingers as he buried his hands in the golden waves…

He was staring again. He met her eyes. Sparkling blue. Dancing.

Good morning," Rose said at last. "Myrta says you made breakfast."

Taurin snapped his attention back to the eggs. "Yes, I… I hope you don't mind."

"Not at all. I love your cooking."

He smiled. "Good. I'll cook for you often, then."

Rose took a step closer. "I would like that."

He stepped toward her, his gaze falling to her pink lips.

"Your eggs are burning." Myrta's sharp voice pierced the air.

Taurin coughed and turned back to the stove. He removed the pan and divided the eggs onto three plates. He put a thick slice of bread on each and served them at the table.

The conversation was sparse and awkward with Myrta there, throwing in a sharp comment every time Taurin and Rose started to talk about anything that wasn't superficial.

Taurin smiled at Myrta. He understood how hard it must be for her to settle in to a new home and a new way of life, but it seemed like she was intentionally trying to keep Rose from being comfortable. He couldn't imagine why Rose was such a devoted friend.

Unless it wasn't Myrta. Maybe it was this place that Myrta hated. Or him.

Well, he couldn't help that. And he wouldn't let Myrta make Rose miserable, either. He just had to find a way to get Rose alone, away from her friend, and then he'd do everything in his power to make sure she never wanted to leave.

90

The Third Son

Tristyn winced at the sound of a shriek echoing down the hallway. A moment later, a herd of his little brothers thundered around the corner, racing toward the courtyard. Tristyn pressed against the wall and waited for them to pass. The nurse gave him an apologetic shrug as she righted a candelabra that the boys had sent teetering as they charged past.

"Make sure to have them clean and quiet in time for the wedding," Tristyn instructed the nurse.

She curtsied. "Yes, Highness. That's why I'm letting them run now."

Tristyn nodded. He remembered tiring himself out beforehand so he could sit through many a dreary event when he was younger. He thought of the pretty chamber maid that cleaned his room and considered burning some energy of his own, but quickly thought better of it. His father would kill him if he didn't answer his summons immediately.

He waited until the boys were out of sight before continuing toward the great hall. If his mother did one thing well, it was producing heirs. After making the mistake of birthing a girl first, she'd made up for it by bearing nine more, all boys. Now, Tristyn's sister was performing the only function suitable for a noblewoman, even if she was the firstborn daughter of a king—an advantageous marriage.

She would marry a prince—a younger brother like himself, not an heir, but a prince nonetheless—and bridge the hostilities between

Sunnland and Cadalania. The king had negotiated the treaty with the ambassador, a weasely little man called Pridte, just a few days before.

Not that Tristyn had room to judge. As the fourth child, his destiny was not much better. Find a wife with as much rank, property, and political clout as possible. Strengthen his father's—and ultimately his brother's—reign. And, if he was lucky, live in comfort and relative happiness in the process.

Tristyn pushed open the door to the great hall. His father stood at the far end of the room, rubbing a tiny piece of paper between his fingers. He looked up when Tristyn entered. "Tris. Good. Tell me, what do you know of Legerdemain?"

Tristyn pulled a chair out from the long table and sat. "Not much. It's a small kingdom, largely self-contained. It lies in the valley surrounded below the Soulless Mountains, and thus it is not really on the way to anywhere, so it's not a hub for commerce or travel. They grow their own crops, manufacture a pretty significant portion of their own goods. Their biggest export is gemstones."

"And therein lies the appeal," the king said. "The kingdom itself will be easy to maintain, simply because it's so small and inexperienced. But having access to those mines…"

"Rumor is that the mines are drying up."

The king shook his head. "Just rumors. I have it on good authority that those mountains hold untold wealth. They just need someone who is willing to dig a little deeper."

"Someone like you."

The king smiled.

"What are you thinking?" Tristyn asked. "An alliance? Gyntor is already betrothed to the princess of the Western Islands. We need her as queen to strengthen our trade routes. And I thought you were hoping for Ryfel to forge an alliance with the barbarians. You don't mean me?"

The king nodded, a grin stretching over his face. "Yes, but not in the way you think. My spies report that Legerdemain is on the verge of collapse. I don't want an alliance with Legerdemain. I want the whole country. And I want you to get it for me."

Tristyn choked. "How?"

"Legerdemain is only a little further north than Cadalania. You will take a company of soldiers to escort your sister to her new home. You will use her hospitality to form your outpost, and from there, it is just a short trip to Legerdemain. With the civil unrest they're already experiencing, securing the country should be an easy feat."

Tristyn grunted. His idea of "easy" differed greatly from his father's.

The king came close and put a hand on Tristyn's shoulder. "I don't care how you do it. If you choose to use force or endear yourself to the people by marrying a local—it doesn't matter to me. But if you succeed in securing Legerdemain for Sunnland, I will make you regent, and your descendants will rule that land after you."

Tristyn's blood pounded through his veins. He'd imagined life as a nobleman. A dignitary in a foreign land. A diplomat, even, regarded by the king of some distant land as an ambassador, trusted to guide them through the intricacies of foreign politics. But a regent? Ruling a kingdom of his own and having a heritage to pass to his children? It was more than he'd ever dared hope for.

He stood and bowed before his father. "I will not fail you. Legerdemain will be ours."

Raid

Rose paced the cabin, scrubbing and rescrubbing every surface, gathering herbs and letting them dry over the fire, pounding them into powder, mixing ointments and tinctures and pastes, and then scrubbing again. She'd been a bundle of nervous energy all day, and all the previous day.

Ever since Taurin and his band had ridden out to rob the caravan.

She helped Myrta wash linens and tear clean cloths into strips for bandages, then went down by the creek to look for quartz and other stones that were good for channeling magic. She went into the village to the small mercantile for more jars to store herbs and the concoctions she made from them three times, the over the two days, and when she got home the last time, she scrubbed some more.

Late on the second evening, Taurin and his band returned.

Rose opened her door to the flood of wounded men and women.

Taurin stumbled in last, covered in dirt and blood, carrying a young man on his shoulders.

"Taurin! Are you…"

"I'm fine," Taurin said, "but Maury is badly wounded."

"Set him on the table," Rose said.

Taurin was back. Safe. And now she had something to do. Her hands stopped shaking and she poured her energy into her work.

She cut the bloody tunic from Maury and removed the wad of blood-soaked cloth Taurin had used to slow the bleeding, exposing a gaping hole in his side.

Her heart sank.

She looked at Taurin, tears stinging her eyes. "Taurin, I…"

Taurin nodded, his eyes red and moist. "I know," he whispered.

The sight of him, all his strength and humor replaced with tears, tied Rose's heart into knots. "I will do what I can. At the least, I can take away the pain."

Taurin nodded. "How can I help?"

"There's hot water on the stove. Keep at least two pots on at all times so I always have clean, hot water."

Myrta came close and handed Rose wet cloths and jars of herbs as she asked for them. Then took the blood-soaked cloths and put them in a bucket to soak and repeated the process as long as Rose worked.

Rose took the first pot and a wet cloth to wash the wound. It was deep, and he'd already lost a lot of blood.

She pointed to one of the jars and told Taurin, "Make that into tea, and force him to drink it."

When the wound was clean, she treated it with an herbal paste, like the one she'd used for Quentyn, but stronger. It would numb the pain and help with healing. If he lived long enough for it to work.

Then she sewed the wound closed and pulled out her quartz. She placed the rocks around the wound and closed her eyes. Concentrating all her energy, she pulled on the magic that swirled in the air and pulsed through the trees, drawing it into the stones and directing it into Maury's body.

She could feel the healing trying to work, but it wasn't enough.

"My cloak," she said.

"What?" Taurin asked.

"My cloak, in my room. Grab it."

Taurin hurried to her room and returned a moment later with the cloak.

Rose took hold of the amethyst clasp and yanked it free of the velvet. She placed it directly on top of the wound and pulled the magic into it, through it.

At last, she released her pull on the magic and took a deep breath. "That is all I can do. He is out of pain, and he should wake up soon, but the damage… It can't be repaired."

Taurin pulled her into an embrace. "Thank you."

The rest of the wounds sustained by Taurin's band were mostly superficial. A few cuts needed stitches, one broken arm needed to be set, but otherwise, there were mostly scratches and bruises that would heal naturally, but more quickly with the help of Rose's ointments.

Finally, everyone was gone except for Taurin.

Thank you for your help tonight," Rose said to Myrta. "You should get some rest."

Myrta nodded and disappeared into the back room.

Taurin stood by Maury's side and lightly touched his forehead. "I told him to stop. The plan was to infiltrate the caravan one at a time. We were dressed like them, and we claimed to be mercenaries, hired to protect the caravan through the mountains. We were going to take just enough to turn a profit."

Rose pulled out a chair for him to sit in and started a pot of tea. "Tell me about him."

"I met him when he was ten. He was a thief, running around picking pockets in the wealthier areas of Nynthavin. I happened to be there when he got caught. I convinced the magistrate he was my son, and the bag of coins he had was mine, and that his accuser was lying. I brought him here, so he wouldn't get caught in the city again."

"That was kind of you," Rose said.

Taurin gave her a half-hearted smile. "I took care of him as best I could. Trained him to be part of my band."

Rose sat beside him and linked her arm with his. He took her hand and intertwined his fingers with hers. "Maury always had to do a little bit more. One more purse, cut from a merchant's belt on our way out of the city. One more minute, every time we're preparing to go anywhere. One more grab, just so he could brag that he'd gotten the most. He spotted a chest, heavily guarded, too big to carry, but he insisted he could get it. The rest of us were all ready to sneak away with our spoils, and he made a run for it."

Maury stirred and blinked. He opened his eyes, and his gaze settled on Taurin. "I... I'm sorry," he whispered. "Should've listened."

"Shh," Taurin soothed. "It's fine now. You're safe."

Maury shook his head. "I wanted... something special. To give you, if..." Maury looked to Rose, then back at Taurin. "You always took care of me. I should've been... better... son."

His eyes fluttered closed.

Rose felt his neck. His heartbeat slowed, then stopped.

She turned to face Taurin.

"He's gone, isn't he?"

Rose nodded.

Taurin pulled her into his arms and held her for a long time, silently sobbing into her hair.

Prisoner

Jyn stalked her brother down the long hallway. "Stoke, please! You must speak with the king for me."

Stoke ignored her and kept walking.

"I have done everything he asked. I have given him the information he needs. There is nothing more I can do. My part has been played out. It's time for him to keep his promise to me and pardon me and Taurin."

Stoke turned a corner and continued walking. "I do not control the king."

"But he listens to you. I'm no longer useful to him, and he knows it, yet he refuses to fulfill his end of the bargain. I need that pardon."

Stoke sighed. "I've told you, the king is not willing to give the pardon until the alliance with Legerdemain is secured. That will happen when Prince Tristyn finds the missing princess."

"It isn't my fault the princess is missing. Why must I be held responsible for the welfare of a foreign princess? For all I know, she's not missing at all. Maybe she's just giving birth to some guard's bastard and they're keeping her hidden until after her confinement. At any rate, that's not my responsibility, nor is it my duty to ensure the peace treaty goes through. I did as the king asked. I spied. I uncovered conspiracies. I confirmed rumors. Why will he not keep his promise?"

Stoke whirled around to face her. "If you're in such a hurry, why don't you put your incredible spying powers to work figuring out what happened to the princess of Legerdemain? Or sit and be patient. At any rate, stop bothering me. I have a prisoner to interrogate." He pushed open a door and strode down the staircase toward a man tied to a chair in the center of the main room of the dungeon.

Jyn gasped.

Gorym?

She ran all the way back to her chamber. When she'd finished her role as Princess Jinna of the Silver Shores, the king had moved her from her opulent suite to a bare, stone servant's room off the kitchen. She was no longer allowed to spend time in her apartment in the city, either. She'd managed to steal some of Princess Jinna's fine clothes, though, and she quickly traded her breeches for a wispy, form-fitting blue gown.

She tiptoed past the kitchen, avoiding the notice of the cooks, and made her way to the wine cellar. She chose a bottle of fine Cadalanian wine and snuck back out past the kitchen and toward the guards' station at the entrance to the dungeon.

The guard on duty was one she'd seen leering at her a few times.

Good.

She snuck into a closet and waited until Stoke emerged from the dungeon, his clothes spattered with blood.

She choked back her anger and waited until she was calm before venturing out of the closet and to the guards' station. She flopped against the door, pretending to be already drunk.

"I found this bottle just lying around, and I need someone to share it with me. When do you get off?"

The guard stared at her, mouth open, for several seconds before answering. "Not for several hours. But why wait? I could spare a moment for a few sips. Come on in."

Jyn hiccupped. "In there? We'll be seen."

He rubbed his chin.

Jyn sighed. "Never mind. I'll find someone else to drink with me."

She turned.

"Wait! I have an idea. There's a room downstairs where the guards sometimes sleep between shifts if it's too far to go home. There's no one in there now."

Jyn beamed at him. "Brilliant. I knew I could count on you." She draped an arm around his neck. "As long as you don't lock me up for too long."

The guard's mouth opened, and he quickly sucked back the saliva that threatened to spill out over his lip.

Jyn blinked slowly, trying to blot out that image, hoping it just reinforced the charade of drunkenness.

The guard unlocked the door to the dungeon. He glanced around to make sure no one was watching, then led her inside. She followed him down the stone stairs. Fresh blood glistened on the floor in the flickering torchlight. She held her breath against the stench until the guard led her around the corner to the small room.

Jyn broke the seal on the wine. "Do you have cups?"

The guard produced two cups from a small cupboard and Jyn sloshed wine into them.

The guard took a swig and stepped closer. Jyn allowed his arm to snake around her waist and pull her close.

Above them, the door to the dungeon creaked open. "Guard! Why aren't you at your post?" Stoke's voice.

Perfect.

The guard swore. "Stay here. Don't move or you'll be seen." He dashed from the room and up the stairs. "I heard a noise, sir. Came down to check on the prisoners."

"And?" Stoke asked.

"All secure."

"Good. Get out parchment. I need you to write down the terms of the last arrest for the logs."

The door to the dungeon clanged shut.

Jyn took a deep breath. She just hoped Stoke would keep the guard long enough for her to do what she came for. She padded softly down the long row of cells, peering in through the bars at the top of each door at the prisoners.

About half of the cells were occupied. Dirty, bruised men in tattered clothes, left here to rot for Nyn knew how long. In the very last cell at the end of the hallway, she found the one she was looking for.

"Gorym!" she hissed.

A pair of hands, followed by a face, appeared in the small window. "Jyn? What are you doing here?"

"I was going to ask you the same thing."

"I was arrested for sorcery."

Jyn clapped a hand over her mouth. After a long moment, she let it fall. "Do they have any proof?"

102

"Do they need it?"

Jyn bit her lip. "When is your trial?"

"They have no intention of giving me a trial. The only reason they're keeping me alive is because they think I can help them. Jyn… they're after Taurin."

Jyn's throat clenched. "What? Why?"

"They heard a rumor from an innkeeper that he may have been in the company of a woman they're looking for."

"A woman?"

The realization hit Jyn like a cannonball to her gut. Of course. The yellow-haired eel she'd seen at Taurin's apartment was the missing princess.

"How did I not hear of this?" she asked.

"Your brother knows you'd never betray Taurin. The only reason they haven't killed you yet is because they might need to use you as leverage to get him to talk."

Jyn clenched her fists. "The only reason I haven't escaped is because the king promised me and Taurin both a pardon."

"I suspect that's what he's counting on. If I were you, I'd get out while he still thinks you believe him."

"What about you?"

Gorym leaned his head against the bars. "They'll torture me until they decide I have nothing left to tell, and then they'll execute me."

"Can't you use magic to escape?"

Gorym shook his head. "The king outlaws magic use by the populace, but he still has magical barriers put on the cells. Ironically, the only way to get out is the old-fashioned way—with the key. If I could get out of my cell, and if I had some supplies, I could spell the guards so they wouldn't be able to see me or track me, but I can't budge the lock on the door."

"I can get the key and take care of the guard. If I get you out, can you get us both out of the palace?"

Gorym nodded.

"What supplies will you need?"

Gorym recited a list.

Jyn took a deep breath. "Be ready. I'm not sure when I'll be able to get everything together, but be assured, I'll come back and we'll escape together. Just don't give them any useful information until then."

103

Deception

Jyn waited in the guard's room, sprawled out on the little cot, until the guard returned from chronicling Gorym's arrest with Stoke.

He touched her arm.

She sat up as though she'd dozed off. She smiled. "There you are."

She took a swig of wine and danced her fingers over his chest. "Where were we?"

The guard chugged his whole glass, then climbed onto the bed, on all fours above her. She let him kiss her and paw her for awhile before pushing him away. "I should be getting back."

The guard groaned. "Must you?" He leaned in again, slobbering on her neck.

"If I'm disciplined by the king, I won't be able to come back at all."

That made him pause long enough for her to slide out from underneath him.

She smoothed her dress. "When are you on shift again?"

"The day after tomorrow."

She smiled. "I'll see you the day after tomorrow, then. Hopefully without so many interruptions."

She turned and hurried up the stairs, leaving him still recovering on the cot. She peeked out the door and, seeing that the way was clear, hurried back to her room to change.

That night, Jyn took a walk through the royal gardens, collecting as many of the herbs Gorym had requested as she could find. She found the type of crystal rock Gorym had told her was a good conduit for magic. Real crystals were better, but if she couldn't get away to the market, she wanted something that would work.

She tucked everything she gathered in a small pouch and hid it at the top of the small set of shelves that her clothes were stacked on, behind a stack of underclothes. Then, she made a stack of her extra trousers and blouses, leaving them on the shelves so they'd be inconspicuous in case Stoke checked her room, but ready for her to shove in a bundle so she could leave in a hurry.

The next morning, she went to find her brother. "I have a lead. I need to go to the marketplace. I have a contact there who will be able to confirm whether or not what I heard is true."

Stoke eyed her. "The marketplace? Are you sure you'll be... safe?"

Safe. She knew exactly how worried he was about her safety.

She gave him an exaggerated eye-roll. "Send a guard if you're that worried. I should only be gone a few hours. I'll need some money, though. I'll need to buy a few things at inflated prices. Information isn't cheap."

Stoke exhaled. "Fine." He handed her a bag of coins and assigned a guard to accompany her, and as Jyn left the palace, she noticed another one following at a distance. Smart. Having her followed in case she slipped away from the first guard.

At least she only had to continue this charade for another day.

She made her way to the marketplace and went straight to the herbalist's shop. The guard started to follow her inside.

She glared at him. "Do you mind? She's not likely to tell me anything if you're standing over my shoulder."

The guard grunted and stood outside the doorway.

Jyn pocketed most of the money Stoke had given her, then purchased the remaining items on Gorym's list.

She knew the guard would be spying, so as she paid, she leaned in close to the shopkeeper and spoke in a low whisper. "That man has been keeping me at arm's length long enough. A pregnancy will make him marry me, good and proper."

The shopkeeper stifled a smile as she looked over the herbs. "Well chosen. Although you may want some of this, as well." She handed Jyn a small jar of something powdered.

"Oh? This is potent?"

The shopkeeper nodded and crooked her finger.

Jyn leaned in closer. "This one is more for him than you. It will make him… more eager to participate. But it won't hurt you, either, so just stir it in the stew. You'll be expecting in a month, you have my guarantee."

Jyn smiled. "I can't thank you enough." She gave the shopkeeper an extra couple montar.

The shopkeeper winked. "You have a good day now, ma'am."

Jyn strode from the shop.

"The palace is the other way," the guard said.

"I must have gotten turned around," Jyn said, continuing in the direction she had started.

"Hey now, where do you think you're going?"

Jyn turned on him. "I have another stop to make. You're just supposed to be protecting me, not dictating where I go."

There. That should convince her brother she was still acting like herself, not behaving in a suspicious manner.

She stalked down the rows of shop tents until she arrived at the gem trader's store.

He smiled when he saw her. "Greetings, m'lady. What can I do for you today?"

Jyn browsed the cases of gems until she found a crystal, a large one that sparkled in the afternoon sun. She pointed to it and he handed it to her. Jyn dug through her pouch of coins and handed the trader twice what it was worth. She leaned in close. "I need you to do me a favor. If anyone asks, particularly someone sent by the king, confirm that you told me a rumor you heard about a man and a golden-haired woman hiding in a tavern at the north end of town last week."

The man glanced at the coins in his hand. His eyes glinted and he looked at her. "That's a lot to remember. I don't do so well when I'm questioned by the king's men."

Jyn handed him another handful of coins.

"Ah, yes, I know the man and woman you're talking about. Heard a rumor about them. Hiding, they are. North end of town."

106

Jyn smiled and gave him a couple more coins. "Thank you for that valuable information. I'll be seeing you."

There were only a few coins left in the bag. Enough that Stoke wouldn't ask why she'd spent so much, despite the handful stashed in her pockets to aid her getaway.

She stalked past the guard on her way out of the trader's shop. "What are you waiting for? We've got to get back to the palace before curfew."

The guard trailed her, and she hurried back to the palace and straight to Stoke's office.

She tossed the leftover coins at him. "I confirmed the rumor I'd heard. I did as you suggested, and I have it on good authority that a woman matching the princess's description was seen in a tavern on the north end of town as recently as last week."

Stoke eyed her.

"Last week? Are you certain?"

Jyn nodded. "She was with a man and another woman. I'll know more in a couple days. My contact in the marketplace is sending someone to check if they're still there, and then he'll contact me. Tell the king to prepare my pardon. I'll have his princess before the end of the week."

That much, at least, was true.

Not that she'd give the princess to Stoke or the king. They had betrayed her, and she wouldn't give them the chance to do it again. But, knowing the princess's actual whereabouts would be valuable currency at some point.

Stoke glanced from the bag of coins to Jyn. "This is good work, Jyn. If it's true and the princess is found, you'll have your freedom."

Nyn's backside, he was almost as good a liar as she was.

Still, she forced a smile to her face, one that she would've worn if she'd believed him.

The next morning, she dressed in another revealing gown, then threw her regular clothes into a bag and hid it behind a flour sack in the kitchen. She stuck the pouch of supplies for Gorym between her breasts and stole another bottle of wine before making her way to the dungeon.

True to his promise, the guard she'd seduced before stood on duty.

He grinned when he saw her. "I was afraid you might not come back."

Jyn lowered her lashes and smiled. "That was silly of you. Can you get away for a short while?"

The guard nodded, fumbling at his waist for the keys. "Stoke has already been to interrogate the prisoner, so he won't be back today."

Jyn hid her fear that it was too late behind a flirtatious smile. "Come on, then."

She traipsed down the stairs and into the little room. She filled the glasses with wine and dumped a packet of powder into the one she gave the guard.

She sat on the cot and patted the spot next to her. Raising her glass, she said, "To a little bit of fun in the midst of this dreary life."

He drank heartily and she filled his glass again.

A few moments later, he slumped over on the cot, his arm lolling over her. She squeezed out of his embrace, replaced the glasses in the cupboard, and placed the bottle on his chest so it would look as though he'd stolen the wine and was drinking alone.

With luck, Stoke would be so focused on the theft of the wine, he wouldn't notice she and Gorym were gone until much later.

She snatched the guard's keys and jogged to the end of the corridor.

"Gorym?"

"I'm here."

"Are you all right?"

He shuffled to the door. "As well as can be expected."

"Can you walk?"

He nodded. "I'll survive."

She unlocked the door and half-carried him down the hallway. She tossed the keys onto the guard's stomach, then slowly made her way up the stairs with Gorym. She hid him in a closet and handed him the pouch of magic supplies while she retrieved her bag from the kitchen.

"The spell is almost ready," Gorym said when she returned. "Are you ready to go?"

She nodded.

He spoke an incantation over the mixture of herbs. The crystal glowed a faint pink color, and a moment later, a cloud formed, growing into a bubble that surrounded them.

Jyn gaped at it. "What does it do?"

"It makes us invisible. No one will see or hear us leave."

They crept from the closet, right out the front of the palace, through the courtyard and out the front gates without so much as a dog barking at them. Gorym kept the shield up until they reached the outskirts of the city.

"Thank you," Gorym said, grasping her hand.

She smiled. "Thank you. Both for the information and for getting me out without being seen. Why don't you come with me to the camp? You'd be welcome there. And we could certainly use a Healer."

Gorym shook his head. "Thank you, but no. I need to get further away than that. Out of the king's jurisdiction. I'm told Zyan welcomes magic users."

Zyan. Even the name evoked a sense of wonder and longing. The land of peace and prosperity, where artisans thrived and everyone was treated as equal. Zyan would be an ideal place to start over. Taurin could be convinced, she was certain of it.

"Can we come with you?"

Gorym squeezed her hand, which he still held. "I owe you a great debt, Jyn. I have a brother in the north, in the village of Wyntley, almost at the edge of Sunnland. I will wait there for one week, but after that, I can make no promises."

Jyn nodded. "I understand. I hope to see you in a week. But if not, safe travels, and if I am ever in Zyan, I will find you."

They embraced, and Gorym took the road that led north, while Jyn headed west. Toward the mountains. Toward Taurin.

The Wedding

Jyn gave the call to alert the sentries to her presence. A return call sounded from the tall rocks that bordered the pass into the valley.

Jyn took a deep breath as she crested the hill that overlooked the Valley of Thieves. Home. At least, it was now. And somewhere down there, Taurin.

She urged her horse forward, toward Taurin's apartment above the bakery. If she couldn't convince Taurin to leave with her, perhaps she'd get a little cabin of her own.

Taurin wasn't home. She left her supplies and clothes on the cot she slept on when she stayed, dropped her horse at the stable, and went in search of him.

Her first stop was the tavern.

"Jyn! You're back!" the buxom wench, Lyndi, grinned. Lyndi had always been a tavern wench, not a criminal, but when her betrothed had killed a man in a fight and gone into hiding, she followed. The two now ran the little village's one tavern.

"I just got in."

"Bring anything pretty with you?"

Jyn winked. "I may have pilfered some gems from a few foreign dignitaries. Have you seen Taurin?"

"Oh, he's probably up at the Healer's house. That's where he spends most of his time these days."

Jyn raised an eyebrow. "The Healer?"

Lyndi nodded. "She and her friend came with him when he came back last time. I must say, having a Healer in the village has been goddess sent. Just last week, two of the boys got injured in a raid, and she patched them right up. She knows her stuff. And her friend has taken up the role of laundress. She charges more than I'd like, but she does a good job and it is nice not to have to wash all the linens myself."

"Where is the Healer's house?" Jyn asked.

"She's renting Quentyn's cabin in the woods, by the stream."

Jyn clenched her teeth. She'd wanted that cabin, but Quentyn's asking price was more than she could afford. She smiled at Lyndi. "Thank you."

The sound of laughing and pleasant chatter greeted her before she even came within sight of the cabin. She was so focused on getting there, she almost missed the young woman outside, scrubbing clothes in a large tub.

The woman glared at Jyn. No, not at Jyn. She was just glaring. Jyn gave her a half-hearted smile as she passed, and trotted up the stairs to the porch. She knocked, but only as a courtesy, before stepping in the open door.

"Hello? Taurin?"

"Jyn!" Taurin jumped up from a table where he'd been sitting with the blonde woman she'd seen at his apartment and hurried to embrace Jyn. His touch was affectionate, but there was something different. Something missing. She couldn't quite determine what it was.

"What have you been up to? I expected you back weeks ago," Taurin said.

"Unexpected business."

"Well, I'm glad you made it back. You remember Rose?" Taurin reached for the woman's hand. "She's the one who Healed me after my injury."

"I remember. You're the Healer here now, I understand."

Rose nodded shyly. "I suppose I am."

Jyn nodded, struggling to keep her features calm and polite. "I'm sure it will be a wonderful benefit to our village to have you here." She turned to Taurin. "Can we talk?"

"I can't right now. I promised Rose I'd help her build an apothecary shelf and collect herbs to stock her stores before winter. How about tonight? At the dance at Lyndi's?"

Jyn smiled through gritted teeth. "I'll see you then."

She stalked from the cabin. The woman outside looked about like Jyn felt.

###

Jyn dressed in one of the gowns she'd gotten from the king in her role as Princess Jinna. One that showed off her figure to the hilt. She traced her features in cosmetics, highlighting her eyes and lips to the fullest effect she knew. She dabbed an aphrodisiatic scent to her neck and wrists. She was as ready as she could get.

She swept into Lyndi's tavern, drawing the eyes of everyone there.

Everyone except Taurin. His eyes remained fixed on Rose. He scarcely spared a glance for Jyn in all her finery. Even dancing with every other man in the room failed to capture his notice, let alone pique his jealousy the way it once would've.

After a few dances, Taurin leapt onto a chair and banged a spoon against a tin cup. "Pardon me, everyone, but I'd like to take a moment to add to the festivities. Rose and I have decided to get married."

Jyn almost choked on her ale. *Married?* For years, Taurin had claimed he'd never get married. That his was not a life he'd impose on any woman. Jyn had been content to be the most important woman in his life, even if he'd never commit to her. And now he was planning to marry this woman he'd only known a couple months?

"We've asked the cleric," Taurin said, nodding toward the man who'd been forced from service to the king for refusing to perform an ancient sacrifice that was supposed to ensure wealth, "and he has agreed to perform the ceremony tonight."

The sound of gagging nearby caught Jyn's attention. She glanced behind her to see Rose's friend, red-faced, clenching and unclenching her fists.

Rose joined Taurin atop the chair and smiled. "I am so thankful to you all for welcoming me into your band. And I would be remiss if I didn't give special thanks to my dearest friend, Myrta, for without her I never would've met Taurin." She smiled up at Taurin.

"Let's begin," the cleric said.

He recited a simple ceremony and performed a basic binding ritual, and a few moments later, declared the act complete.

Taurin kissed Rose, right there in front of everyone.

112

Jyn glanced at Myrta. "I see you are as pleased by this turn of events as I am," she said in a low tone.

Tears threatened to spill from Myrta's eyes. "I gave up everything for her. I had a good job in a lavish castle. I was respected for my station. I helped her escape and saved her life more times than I can count, and for what? I'm a... a washerwoman in a camp of criminals, while she is the most respected person in town, and married to one of the band's leaders."

Jyn nodded. "I have done the same for him. Waited endlessly, his best and truest friend, only to have him lose his mind the first time someone else came along."

"I hate him," Myrta said. "I hate them both."

"Perhaps there's something we can do about it," Jyn said.

For the first time since Jyn had seen her that morning, something other than anger glinted in Myrta's eyes. Excitement. "What do you have in mind?"

Making Plans

Jyn and Myrta walked through the woods by the creek. Myrta's face reflected how Jyn felt, with her jaw set in a firm line, eyes flashing.

"They said I could stay with them," Myrta spat. "Can you believe it? Living in the front room, like a servant, while they're in back..." She crushed a leaf in her hand. "We were supposed to be equals. When we left. But she will never think of me as anything more than her servant."

Jyn nodded. "I gave up the sea for him. He was captured by the royal navy, and I attacked the ship to get him out. My ship was destroyed in the process, and he convinced me not to rebuild. Told me to stay, and we could work together. I knew he thought of me as something like a sister, but I always thought, someday..."

She tossed a stick in the creek and watched it float away. Like a pirate ship. "I was the only woman in his life for so long. The only one he trusted. I thought one day he'd realize I'm the one who has always been there, the one who always would be there. But it's too late now."

Myrta nodded. "She's pregnant. I don't think she even realizes it yet, but I've been caring for her so long, I saw the signs immediately."

Jyn frowned. "That complicates matters. I have no wish to harm a child, even their child."

"Perhaps revenge doesn't have to be against them personally. She left her country because she loves it. She believed her leaving would somehow save it. If something were to happen to her homeland, it would devastate her far more than death."

Jyn kicked a pile of fallen leaves and pulled her cloak a little tighter. "You would take down an entire nation just to hurt her?"

Myrta scowled. "I thought you wanted revenge, too. If you're backing out now..."

"No, that's not it at all. I think it's brilliant. I admire anyone brave enough to think big. How would we do it?"

Myrta shrugged. "I'm not sure yet. I was hoping you'd have a plan. You're the one with experience in international intrigue. But I grew up in the palace. I can tell you anything you want to know. I know the castle, the servants, the customs Why, I know Rose so well I could practically be her."

Jyn stopped and put a hand on Myrta's arm. "What did you say?"

Myrta stared at her for a long moment before her face broke into a wide smile. "You have a plan."

"Oh, I have a plan," Jyn grinned. "One that will get us everything we want, and it will give me a chance to get some revenge of my own."

The Search

Ada eyed the amulet that hung around the king's neck. A pale glow throbbed slowly, not bright enough to attract any attention but hers. The princess was in trouble.

The princess's maid had sent a letter from the inn, saying the princess had fallen ill and was being cared for there. She sent another letter every day, saying the princess's condition continued to improve, but she needed to stay at the inn. After a week, the king sent his personal physician, only to discover the maid had left a stack of letters and instructions to deliver one per day, while Anarosia and her maid had run off with the merchant caravan. The king had sent men, of course, but by the time they caught up to the caravan there was no telling where the girls were.

But now the amulet throbbed. The pulse of the kingdom, bound to the royal line, signaled to Ada that something threatened the princess.

Ada hobbled across the great throne room and stood before the king. "A word, your majesty? In private?"

"Of course," the king said. He stood and led the way to the private room just off the throne room.

Ada shuffled after him, leaning heavily on her walking stick. "You must let me go after the princess. She is in trouble."

"What kind of trouble? How do you know?"

"I always know. I can attempt to See, if you would like, although my attempts in the past have been thwarted, but I know I can find her."

The king shook his head. "I can't allow it. I have men searching for her. I received word just this morning that she was sighted in a small village on the edge of Sunnland a few weeks ago, and she may be headed for Nynthavin."

"Then that's where I'll start."

"Ada. You know I trust your counsel, but you are not fit for a journey like this. You could be set upon by brigands at any point. You could fall off your saddle and be injured, or…"

"I assure you, I'm more fit than I look. Send with me a small company of soldiers. I will be fine. Your men will not find her. Only I can."

The king rubbed his chin. "How?"

Ada pointed to the amulet. "It will lead me to her."

"Are you sure? You can bring her home safely?"

"I can make no guarantees. But I can find her. She is still alive, but she is in danger. I must leave immediately."

The king's chest rose and fell with a deep breath.

"Very well. You may depart at dawn." He removed the amulet from around his neck.

"I'll expect you to bring both this and my daughter safely back to me."

Ada bowed, as far as her stiff back would allow.

The next morning, just as the sun rose over the forest to the east, Ada and her company of soldiers rode out from the palace, making as much haste as they could, knowing they had several days of hard travel ahead.

After a few days, they came upon a small village in Kirland. While the soldiers asked the same questions as the soldiers before them had, Ada stood at the crossroads and held the amulet in her hands.

"The innkeeper said the caravan traveled east toward Cadalania and on to Zyan," the head of the guard, Funda, said.

"We will travel southwest, toward Sunnland."

"But, my lady…"

"Trust me. We travel toward Sunnland, with no time to spare."

The amulet pulsed brighter the further southwest they went. It throbbed when they reached the first small village within the Sunnland border.

"The princess was here," Ada said.

117

They spent the night at a small inn, and learned that two finely dressed ladies had traded their gowns for food and had stayed on as tavern maids for several weeks before leaving.

"One was a right good worker," the innkeeper said. "I only kept the other because the first was so useful as to make up for the both of them."

Ada smiled. "The other was not accustomed to labor. She was brought up to lead."

That night, Ada stood facing Nynthavin. They would reach the city the next day, but something wasn't right.

Funda brought his horse up alongside Ada. "I have received a message from home. The king has died, and Parliament suspects a plot by foreign powers. A contingent of Sunnland soldiers, led by a prince, has set up camp outside our borders. Parliament fears they plan to start a war."

The amulet throbbed in Ada's hand.

"What else?" she asked.

"Prince Andro has ascended to the throne in Anarosia's absence. He has sent Prince Amberte to join us in searching for the princess."

The amulet burned Ada's palm. "We must make haste for Nynthavin. The princess is in even greater danger than before."

A Rose

Rose sat up and stretched. Taurin wasn't in bed. She pulled a dress over her head and went into the other room. Taurin looked up from where he knelt, stoking the fire. "Good morning, my love. Breakfast will be ready soon."

"Good. I'm famished. Thank you, dearest."

"This mountain air must agree with you. You've been eating a lot lately."

Rose smiled, then glanced around the cabin. "Myrta hasn't returned yet?"

Taurin shook his head. "I asked at the tavern and no one has seen her or Jyn."

"I don't understand why she would just leave."

Taurin chuckled. "Don't you?"

Rose cocked her head to the side. "Of course I understand *that*. But I would've expected her to stay in town. And if she really wanted to leave, I would've expected her to say something. What if she's hurt somewhere, or in trouble?"

Taurin put a pan of eggs above the fire to oil. "Myrta is one of the most capable women I've ever known. Besides, she's with Jyn. Between the two of them, there's nothing they can't accomplish. I'm sure they're fine."

"I know, it's just…"

"You miss her."

Rose smiled at him. "Yes. I know our wedding was sudden, but I didn't think she'd be so upset that she'd leave."

Taurin came close and kissed her. "Perhaps she just needed some time to adjust. I'm sure Jyn has convinced her to go on a wild adventure, but she'll be back when she's ready."

"I hope so. She's been by my side through so much. There's so much I want to tell her. I'm going to need her."

"That's what you have me for now." Taurin sat on the chair by the table. "Which reminds me. I've been thinking. Now that we're married and I have someone besides myself to think of, I would like to find a new trade."

Rose's heart jumped inside her. She'd been hesitant to bring it up—thieving was all Taurin had ever known—but she worried every time he left on a raid that he wouldn't come back.

She perched on his lap and slid her arms around his neck. "What would you do?"

"I don't know for sure, but I'd like to see if I would be successful as an artisan."

"What do you mean?"

"Once, I robbed a caravan that had a whole wagon of goods from Zyan. Sculptures, jewelry in intricate designs, wood carvings, and so much else. I always wished I could make something myself instead of taking others' things, but for a long time I was so busy trying to survive, I couldn't even consider it. But now…"

Rose caressed his face with her fingertips, memorizing every line around his eyes, the way the stubble on his cheek scratched gently, the love emanating from his eyes. "I think it's a wonderful idea."

"I have something to show you."

Taurin set her on the floor and went into their bedroom. He returned a moment later and handed her a small purple gem in an intricate setting of gold petals that entwined it, wrapping around it in the shape of a rose.

Rose gasped. "This is beautiful! Did you do this?"

Taurin nodded. "It's the amethyst from your cloak. The setting was damaged when you tore it off., the night…" He choked.

Rose grasped his hand. "I thought it had been lost or stolen. I was so busy, anyone could've taken it, but I didn't want to make any accusations."

Taurin smiled. "That was gracious of you." He coughed. "Anyway, I was going to have it repaired, but then I thought... I hope you don't mind. I just thought, that was the night when I knew I was in love with you, and I wanted to do something special for you. So I made a rose for my Rose."

Tears stung Rose's eyes. "It's beautiful, Taurin. As fine as anything any Zyanite could make." She looked at him. "I have something to tell you. I wasn't sure before, but I am now. You see, dearest, we're going to have a baby."

Taurin's delighted shriek filled the cabin. He lifted her in his arms and spun her around. "Oh, my love. I could not be more happy."

Rose smiled. "One more thing."

"Anything for you, my love."

"If it's a boy... I was thinking we could name him Maury."

Taurin pulled her into his arms, and his tears mingled with hers as they held each other for a long moment. He pressed his lips against hers, pouring a lifetime of love into her, promising with that kiss a lifetime more.

Spell

Jyn looked up and down the street in the little village of Wyntley, checking landmarks before determining she was on the right stoop. She knocked on the door.

"Jyn. I didn't think you'd come." Gorym stared out at her from the warmth of the cottage door.

"I didn't think you'd wait."

"I wasn't going to, but the news from the city—where are my manners? Come in, come in." Gorym bustled Jyn and Myrta inside, then peered out the door, up and down the street. "Where's Taurin?"

"He didn't come."

Gorym started to open his mouth, then closed it and showed Jyn and Myrta to chairs by the fire.

"You were about to tell me news?" Jyn said.

"Oh, yes. There's unrest in Cadalania because of a recent treaty with Kirland. It seems the people are not as enthralled by the idea as the nobility are, especially after their prince married the princess of Sunnland, and they're showing their feelings by lashing out at anyone they suspect of being Kirish—which means anyone foreign at all. Including an innocent Healer just trying to pass through on his way to Zyan. So I stayed, hoping the unrest would settle down before the king's soldiers caught up to me."

"Well, I'm glad you did. I need your help."

Myrta sat silently, as Jyn had instructed her to do. Jyn wasn't sure how Gorym would react to her request, and she didn't need Myrta

124

messing things up. Gorym's debt to her should make him willing, but he owed Myrta nothing, and that woman's sharp tone might make him refuse to help at all.

"I owe you my life. What do you need?"

"I need a spell. A powerful one. I need to change the way someone looks."

Gorym tilted his head. "Change whose looks?"

Jyn nodded toward Myrta. "Hers."

Gorym blinked, but his face was otherwise unreadable. "What does she need to change?"

Jyn pulled a paper out of her bag, unfolded it, and passed it to him. "She needs to look like that."

Gorym stared at the picture for a long time.

At last, he looked at her. "Whatever you're up to, I want no part of it."

"I'm not asking you to say anything to anyone or risk yourself in any way. All I need is the spell to change her looks."

"If someone finds out..."

"No one will. But if they did, it would be on me, not you. And, as you mentioned, you owe me."

Gorym sighed. "It will take several days. I'll need to brew a potion to alter her features, and I'll need to create another spell to make her features appear the way you want them to."

Jyn nodded. "Fine. Let me know what supplies you need. I have money."

"You'll need it. This will be difficult and complicated."

"It will be worth it."

"You know why they want her, right?" Gorym nodded toward the picture on the paper. "The king has negotiated a deal. If they help recover her, she has to marry the king's son."

"I know."

Gorym jerked his head in Myrta's direction. "If your girl marries the prince, you'll be allied with the men who imprisoned and betrayed you and then tried to kill you. If she doesn't, he'll go to war with you. Either way, you lose."

"I have a plan."

"You'd better. Let's go to bed. If I'm going to do this, I'd like to get it over with. Uprisings or not, I'm leaving for Zyan as soon as I'm done with you."

The next morning, Jyn wrote two letters. When she finished, she found Myrta, who was still sound asleep in the small room Gorym's cousin had let them use.

Jyn nudged her awake. "Do you have the ring?"

Myrta pulled a ring off her finger. Jyn looked at it. The seal was simple—a triangle with a dragon head in the center. She wondered briefly what it meant as she took it downstairs. She reread her first letter.

I know who you're looking for. I have a plan to get her away from where she is being held. We will meet you in the alley behind The Thorn and Pony Inn at sunset on the evening of the first day of next month, by the Nynite calendar. Signed, a friend.

She rolled the paper and stuck it in a pouch that she kept on the inside of her trousers.

She then looked at the other letter. She'd have to be very careful about that one. It could either deliver her future on a platter or be her undoing.

Prince Marckis, when you met me I was posing as the princess from the Silver Shores. In reality, I was a spy, serving the queen of Legerdemain, trying to uncover plots against our nation. Her Majesty wishes to discuss a treaty between your nation and ours. I will be in further contact to discuss a meeting once Her Majesty is safely out of Sunnland. By the authority of the queen of Legerdemain, Royal Counsel, Jyn.

She rolled the parchment and smeared the wax to seal it, then pressed the ring with the seal Myrta had stolen from Rose to leave the imprint of the symbol.

She hired the most trustworthy people she knew of to deliver the missives—a band of thieves. She promised twice again as much as she paid them if they returned with a response.

Now, all she had to do was hope Gorym knew what he was doing when it came to spellcraft.

The Imposter

"We've found her!"

Ada looked up from her mug of tea at the soldier who had burst into the common room.

"A woman in the market gave this to me." The soldier handed a small scrap of parchment to the prince.

The prince took it and read aloud. "I know who you're looking for. I have a plan to get her away from where she is being held. We will meet you in the alley behind The Thorn and Pony Inn at sunset on the evening of the first day of next month, by the Nynite calendar. Signed, a friend."

The prince took a deep breath. "I hope this is not another beggar, hoping for money."

The amulet throbbed against Ada's chest. Something wasn't right. Not just another dead-end, but something more sinister.

She'd tried Seeing, but some sort of magic blocked her.

The soldiers scurried around, making preparations to meet the letter writer. Ada clutched the amulet, trying to connect to it, to hear what it wanted to tell her, but a vague impression of danger was the most she felt.

They spent the next week at an inn down the street from The Thorn and Pony, awaiting the appointed time.

The night of the meeting, Ada prepared the soldiers and readied an array of magic, in case she needed it.

The lamps that lined city streets did not extend to the alley behind the inn, leaving the space shadowed and dim. Ada stepped carefully to avoid the refuse that littered the cobbled path. She stood near a wall, ignored by the prince and his soldiers, as she had been most of the journey. They trusted in their swords and their wits to win the day, giving no thought to Ada or what she tried to tell them.

Shortly after dusk, two figures, cloaked in robes, came around the corner into the alley.

The prince drew his sword. "Who goes there?"

One of them threw back her hood. "Amberte, it's me."

The woman wore Her Majesty Anarosia's face, but it was not Anarosia. Ada knew as much even before the amulet flared.

The prince sheathed his sword and started toward the woman.

"Stop!" Ada shouted. "It is not the queen. She is an imposter."

"Nonsense," Amberte said. "Do you think I don't know my own sister?" He embraced the woman.

The woman returned the embrace. She looked around Amberte's shoulder, staring directly at Ada with a sinister smile.

Ada knew her, but she couldn't quite place her. She wore Anarosia's face, but it was prettier, somehow. Her features more symmetrical, her eyes larger and framed by darker lashes, her skin smoother and unfreckled.

The woman pulled back and put a hand to Amberte's face. "Who would have thought a few months could make such a difference in my little brother? Where is the boy who used to chase me around the castle with jars of spiders?"

Amberte laughed. "You squealed so delightfully."

The imposter had intimate details of Anarosia's life. How could she know such things, unless…

"Myrta," Ada said aloud.

The imposter jumped.

"What's that?" the prince asked.

"Sadly, Myrta is no longer with us," Myrta said. "My dearest friend died trying to save me from my kidnappers."

"Kidnappers? We thought you ran away," Amberte said.

Myrta nodded. "That's what they wanted you to think. It was an elaborate plot, to hold me hostage until the kingdom was desperate, and then ransom me." She held out a hand to her companion, who came forward and lowered her hood.

"This is my one true friend, Jyn. She is a merchant who had dealings with my kidnappers. She befriended me and promised to help me escape when she could, so when she heard you were looking for me, she made a plan to get me out and bring me to you. She shall be my chief advisor when I am crowned queen."

Ada tried to protest, but no one wanted to listen to an old woman. Myrta's performance as Anarosia was flawless. No one else doubted her identity.

"We must make all haste to return home. I'm sure you've heard by now that father has passed away. Andro is ruling in your absence, but the country needs its queen."

"Yes, let's get away as soon as possible. I don't want to spend another day here." Myrta shuddered, as though she really meant it.

"We must also send a contingent to bring your kidnappers to justice."

Myrta glanced at Jyn, whose jaw hardened, then placed a hand on Amberte's arm. "No, please, brother. They cannot harm me any longer. I just want to go home."

"Very well," the prince said. "We will discuss it further when we get home." He bustled Myrta and her friend Jyn back to the inn where they'd been staying, a much nicer affair than The Thorn and Pony.

Once Myrta and Jyn were tucked into a room at the inn and guards were placed at their door, Ada approached the prince.

"My lord, I know Her Majesty desires to forgive and move forward with her life, and I support her, but such devious plotting must not be allowed to go unpunished. The queen has been missing for months, and such a thing is not to be taken lightly. Nor do we have time to wait to discuss it until we return home. We must find these kidnappers before they have a chance to go into hiding. Please, leave me with a small contingent of soldiers. We can track down the kidnappers while you get Her Majesty to safety."

The prince rubbed his chin. "It is a wise plan. Very well. We'll leave at first light, and I'll leave you to deal with the kidnappers."

The next morning, Ada stood outside the inn as the prince prepared to leave. When Myrta came out, Ada stopped her. "Enjoy it while you can, because very soon, the true queen will be back on the throne."

Myrta smiled, that sly, devious smile. "Even if you find her, which you won't, you won't bring her back. She doesn't want to come.

This way, everyone is happy." She turned away. "I am the queen now, and there is nothing you can do."

"We shall see," Ada said. "We shall see."

The Amulet's Call

One Year Later

Rose woke to the sound of voices shouting. She glanced across the room to where the baby lay, but he hadn't stirred.

The shouts drew closer.

Rose nudged Taurin awake. He stretched, then tensed as another shout jarred the peaceful surroundings.

"Stay with Maury," he said as he drew on his trousers. He hurried out, and Rose sat rigid in bed, clutching the blanket, listening.

"She showed up at the tavern." Lyndi's voice. "Started demanding to see Ana-somebody. Said she knew she'd been there. Must've used magic to get past the patrols."

Rose's heart stilled.

It couldn't be. How had they found her?

"Is she alone?" Taurin asked.

"I have scouts out checking to be sure, but as far as I can tell, yes," Lyndi said.

"Release her," Taurin said. "She's a harmless old woman."

Old woman? It couldn't be... could it?

"She's a witch!" Lyndi said.

Taurin's warm chuckle wafted in. "So is my wife."

Lyndi grunted. "Very well. I'll be right outside if you need me."

Rose got up and stepped into the main room just as Taurin came inside with the old woman.

Rose's heart tripped over itself as her fears were confirmed. "Ada."

Ada bowed, as low as her crooked back would allow. "Your Majesty."

Taurin coughed. "Your Majesty? I knew you were noble, but..."

Rose sighed. "Please sit, Ada. I'll make some tea. It is clear we have much to discuss."

A short time later, Rose sat at the small table with Ada while Taurin hovered protectively behind her.

"How did you find me?" Rose asked.

"It was not easy. I lost track of you in Nynthavin. No amount of bribing or spying or even magic brought me any closer. I stayed for a year, searching every corner of the city. In the end, it was a simple thief in the marketplace. I knew he'd seen you, been close to you. I followed him back here."

"What do you want?"

In answer, Ada pulled a small, cloth-wrapped bundle from a pocket in her cloak and set it on the table. She nudged it toward Rose.

For reasons she couldn't quite define, Rose's heart quickened and sweat slicked her palms. She slowly unwrapped the cloth. Inside, a brilliant purple gem, encased in a gold setting etched with ancient writing, flashed up at her, glowing with an iridescence not attributable to the dim light from the early morning sun coming through the window.

Behind her, Taurin gasped. "That must be worth a fortune."

Ada looked up at him. "More than you know."

Rose scowled. "He's not planning to steal it."

"The idea never entered my mind," Ada said. "He couldn't, even if he wanted to."

Rose lifted an eyebrow, but Ada didn't elaborate.

"Why did you bring it?"

"Because it's yours."

Rose shook her head. "No, it isn't. Not anymore."

"You did not cease to be queen just because you left."

"That's exactly what I did."

"Your kingdom needs you."

"I Saw the future, Ada. The kingdom is better off without me."

"So you will live here, in this den of criminals, while your kingdom dies?"

"My brothers are perfectly capable of ruling without me. They are of the royal bloodline, too."

"That isn't how it works. Not for us." Ada pushed the amulet closer to Rose. It pulsed with light from within. "Do you know what that means? It means you are the rightful queen. When your country was founded, that amulet was imbued with magic. That magic is passed to the firstborn in your line. It is what empowers you to rule. If you die without a child—although I see now that's no longer relevant—but if you had, then the magic could be transferred to another, but as long as you live, it is bonded to you. It calls you. Can't you hear it?"

Rose squeezed her eyes closed so she couldn't see the amulet blazing at her, but she couldn't quiet the steady hum that tugged at her.

"I can't," she whispered. "Don't you see? I can't go back. If I do, the kingdom will suffer far more than you can imagine."

She opened her eyes and rewrapped the amulet in the cloth, careful not to touch it. "Please believe me when I say I would if I could. But I care more about the future of my country than my own desires."

Ada eyed her. "Are you certain you Saw the future you think you Saw?"

"There is no mistaking it. I've relived the nightmares a thousand times." She pushed the bundle back toward Ada.

"Keep it. It is yours."

"It belongs to the kingdom."

"You *are* the kingdom."

"I'm not coming back."

"Then save it. One day, your son will need it to reclaim his heritage." Ada stood slowly and walked toward the door. She paused just before leaving. "I know you're afraid of the future, but if you choose to use the amulet, you might be surprised by what you See."

Rose stared at the doorway for a long time after Ada disappeared.

Taurin sat beside her, taking her hand in his and holding it silently.

Minutes or maybe hours later, Rose's thoughts were broken by the sound of Maury's cry from the next room.

Taurin stood and got the baby, bringing him to her to feed.

"What are you going to do?" he asked finally.

Rose smiled at him. "Nothing. My home is here, with you and Maury. I love this place and these people. I have no desire to leave."

134

"But your kingdom—"

"Is better off without me."

She finished feeding the baby, then handed him to Taurin. She took the cloth-shrouded amulet into the bedroom and tucked it in a hollow space where one of the boards on the wall had come loose. But though it was hidden from sight, she could still feel it pulsing, hear the plaintive croon of its song.

The Kingdom

Jyn handed the treaty to Myrta. "Sign."

Myrta glared at the door Marckis had just left through. "Why did I have to get married?" she whined.

"I explained this already. It legitimizes your role as queen. Maybe in Legerdemain a queen can rule by herself, but the rest of the world sees that as a weakness. If you want to be respected as a leader in this world, you need to be married."

"But why did I have to marry *him*?"

Jyn rolled her eyes. "Because he's the one who could offer you the best treaty. King Wyllym only wanted your alliance in order to take over. Establish a hold here so he could cut off Kirland and Cadalania from each other. Then it would only take a few little wars for him to take over everything. It would only be a matter of time until the whole world became that bastard's slaves. By marrying Marckis, we've developed a stronghold across the entire northern half of the continent."

"How is being Marckis's slave better than being Wyllym's?"

"You're not his slave. I swear, Myrta—"

"Don't call me that!" Myrta hissed. "What if someone hears?"

Jyn gave a mock bow. "My apologies, your Majesty. As I was saying, you just need to trust me. I've gotten you this far, haven't I?"

Myrta gave her a grudging nod.

"We are on equal footing with Kirland, and I have a plan to give us the upper hand. When I'm finished, you'll be free to rule this country by yourself, and I'll be your regent in Kirland."

"My regent?" Myrta's greedy eyes lit up.

"Exactly. Legerdemain will hold Kirland as a vassal state, and you'll be queen, and then you'll send me to rule for you."

"What is this plan? What do I have to do?"

"First, you must solidify your claim. There must be no one else to challenge your rule."

"What do you mean?"

Jyn clenched her teeth. Did she have to spell out every detail for this simpleton? "Anarosia's brothers. You need to execute them."

"Why?"

"Because they already don't trust you, and at any time, one of them could try to steal the throne from you."

"No, I understand that part, I mean, on what grounds do I execute them?"

"I will provide you with proof that they're plotting against you. You'll execute them for treason."

Myrta nodded. "I'll can an assembly this afternoon. Can you have proof for me to show Parliament?""

Jyn smiled. "It's already in place."

"Fine. Anarosia's brothers will be hanged at sunset. What else do I have to do?"

Jyn took a deep breath before responding. "You have to let Marckis get you with child."

Myrta jumped to her feet. "What? No. Absolutely not." She shuddered. "Every time he touches me…"

Jyn slapped her. "Do you think real queens never have to do anything they don't like? If you want to keep this kingdom, you have to produce an heir. Fortunately for you, it doesn't matter if it's male or female. Just have a baby."

Myrta started to open her mouth, but Jyn stopped her before she could start. "But it has to be *his* heir. We can't afford to have anyone raise a question about its legitimacy. It is his child's claim to the throne that will give you the authority to control his kingdom through me. Once the baby is born, we can kill Marckis, but you have to establish your child's claim first."

Myrta glared at her, rubbing the red imprint of Jyn's hand on her face. "Fine. But the second I have that baby, he's going to die a horrible, painful death."

"Deal." Jyn stared her down for a few more seconds, just to remind her who was really in charge, and marched from the room. She strode down the hallway to Prince Marckis's chambers. She glanced around to make sure no one was watching before she slipped inside.

Marckis rose from where he lay on the bed and came to greet her. Slipping his arms around her waist, he kissed her neck, slowly working his way down to her collarbone." "Did she agree?" he murmured between kisses.

"Of course. She's a puppet."

Jyn caught her breath as Marckis lifted her and carried her to the bed. "You have to publicly claim the child," Jyn said. "Send word home announcing your child's legitimacy."

Marckis lay beside her, partially pinning her to the bed, and his kisses turned to soft nibbles. "Of course."

"Then, when she dies tragically shortly after the baby is born, it will be natural for you to return home with your child, and who better to keep your son's kingdom safe for him than the queen's most trusted advisor? From there, it will be simple enough to take Cadalania, and it's only a matter of time before we can destroy Sunnland. Between us, we'll rule the world."

Marckis smiled. He pressed his mouth to hers, kissing her so hard it almost hurt. After a long time, he pulled away slightly and smiled at her. "There is no part of this I'm not going to enjoy."

News

Rose sat up in bed, cold sweat covering her body, her breath coming in shallow gasps.

Taurin sat up beside her, putting his hand on her leg. "What is it, love?"

Though her eyes were open, she could still see flashes of the vision. "My nightmare is back. The one where I order the deaths of my family."

Taurin pulled her into his embrace.

"I don't understand. I haven't had that dream since I've been here. Why would it come back? And why would it feel so real, like it's happening already?"

"Maybe something happened. Something to make that future possible. Maybe you should…"

"No. Seeing is what brought the nightmares in the first place."

Despite her words, her gaze turned to the panel in the wall where the amulet was hidden.

For awhile after Ada had left it with her, she'd been able to ignore it, but lately its throbbing had grown louder, more insistent.

"Rose. You've been restless for weeks. It's only growing worse. Wouldn't it be better if you could know for sure what's happening in your homeland?"

She shook her head and pulled away. "It was just a dream."

She lay back down, as far away from him as the small bed would allow, but couldn't get back to sleep. She fidgeted until Taurin got up and went into the other room to make breakfast.

As soon as she'd given Maury his morning feeding, she dressed him and set him in a small pen in the front room with his wooden toys. Taurin was already at work in the little lean-to he and Quentyn had built for him to use as a workshop. Once a month, Donnin, one of the members of Taurin's band, took a supply of the jewelry Taurin had crafted into the city to sell, bringing back gold and gems for him to use on the next pieces. She ate the breakfast Taurin had left out for her and busied herself mixing herbs into remedies, but her mind lingered back in Legerdemain, where her family screamed in pain and outrage as their executions were carried out. She saw it as clearly as if she were still in the dream.

She had to get out of the house. Away from the amulet. At least for a little bit. She bundled Maury into his warm clothes and poked her head into the workshop. "I'm going into the village for supplies. Do you want to come?"

Taurin stood and brushed the dust from his hands. "With my lovely wife and perfect son? Always." He kissed her, then took Maury, who kicked to be put down.

Rose laughed at her son's insistence on walking without help down the path to the village on his chubby, unsteady legs. He tired after awhile, and Taurin scooped him up. They made their way to the mercantile where Rose bought milk and cheese and vegetables, along with some extra jars.

The door to the mercantile burst open. Lyndi burst in. She scanned the room until her eyes landed on Taurin. "Good, I heard you were here. Donnin is back from the city. He has news." She paused to take a breath. "Of Jyn."

Rose jerked her head around. Beside her, Taurin dropped the clay bowl he'd been examining. It shattered on the floor with a loud crunch.

"Jyn? Is she…?"

"I don't know," Lyndi said. "Donnin is at the tavern. He just said to find you."

Taurin bolted for the door.

141

Rose pressed an extra coin into the shopkeeper's hand. "For the bowl," she said. She scooped Maury and her purchases into her arms and hurried after Taurin.

A small crowd had gathered in the main room of the tavern when she arrived. Donnin stood atop a table, his grin wide, clearly displaying his enjoyment of the attention afforded the bearer of tales.

"Jyn, is she hurt?" Taurin demanded.

"Quite the opposite," Donnin said. "I was talking to one of my contacts within the palace. It seems the king is furious. You see, he had negotiated a treaty with the country of Legerdemain…"

Rose's breath caught in her throat.

"…to have one of his sons wed their queen."

Rose choked.

"But the queen broke their treaty and forged an alliance with Kirland by marrying the prince of that land. And who do you think negotiated that treaty? None other than the queen's most trusted advisor, our very own Jyn!"

A round of cheers echoed around the room, but Rose barely heard them.

"I don't understand," she whispered to no one.

Taurin came to stand beside her and took her hand. "Rose, I know the thought of Seeing again scares you, but you have to stop hiding. It's time you found out what's happening to your home." He took Maury and led Rose back to their cabin.

Rose gathered the herbs she would need through a haze of confusion. Her thoughts shoved one another in circles, trying to make sense of the news.

At last, she was ready.

"Will you take Maury outside?" she asked Taurin. "I need quiet so I can concentrate."

Taurin nodded, and soon the sound of Maury's giggles faded into the sounds of the woods.

She walked slowly to the back room and lifted the wood panel. She hesitated before reaching inside to touch the small bundle hidden there. Its song was louder than ever, reverberating against the inside of her head.

Picking it up, she carried it gingerly to the table. She stared at it for a long time before finally unwrapping it. The amethyst glowed, a purple glare so bright it was almost blinding.

142

Rose closed her eyes and started the process of trying to See for the first time since she'd the vision that had started this whole ordeal.

When the vision ended, she hung the amulet around her neck and went outside. She walked toward the stream, to the shallows where Maury liked to splash.

Taurin stood to face her when she parted the trees and walked toward him, his face expectant.

She took a deep breath. "I need to go home."

Siege

Rose jumped when the door to Taurin's apartment in town banged open.

"Dada!" Maury cooed.

Taurin scooped up their son and sat next to Rose on the bed. "The news isn't good. The king is furious. Apparently he'd been negotiating a treaty with Legerdemain, but Myrta, acting as you, broke the treaty and forged an alliance with Kirland by marrying Kirland's heir apparent, Prince Marckis. They then also allied themselves with Cadalania and have been forcing trade routes through Sunnland to reroute through Legerdemain to Kirland. Sunnland has declared war on Legerdemain, but Legerdemain has Kirland and Cadalania to fight if Sunnland follows through with the war."

Rose's stomach churned. How could Myrta do such a thing? "We have been neutral for hundreds of years. This treaty goes against everything we are."

Maury put an arm around her.

"This is all my fault," she said. "I never should have left. Ada was right—the future I thought I Saw…"

Taurin kissed her. "You couldn't have known. You were trying to protect your kingdom."

Rose wiped a tear from her cheek. "She killed my family."

"And more will die when Sunnland attacks."

Rose breathed deeply. "We'd better get going, then. We have no time to lose."

At dawn the next morning, Rose and Taurin started the long journey toward Legerdemain. They took four horses, each of them riding one with one to spare, trading off periodically so the horses could rest, and taking turns holding Maury in their laps. They rode as fast as the horses could go, stopping only briefly to rest and eat, sleeping at inns if they could find them, or bundling together under layers of blankets outside, despite the crisp, fall air that got colder the further north they traveled, and before long, they left Sunnland behind.

A scout from the Sunnland army stopped them on the road a few miles from the river that encircled Legerdemain. "What is your business in these parts?" he asked.

"We are travelers, headed to Legerdemain," Taurin said.

"I'm sorry, your trip will have to wait. Legerdemain is under quarantine."

Rose lifted an eyebrow. "Quarantine?" Under the bodice of her dress, the amulet thrummed gently.

"I'm sorry, madam, but the risk of the plague spreading is too great. I cannot allow anyone past the border."

"You are not a Legerdemain soldier. You have no authority to deny entrance into the country."

The soldier drew a sword. "I have all the authority I need."

"Enough," another soldier said, riding up from behind the first. "I have instructions to escort you to the prince. This way."

Rose and Taurin followed him through the rows of tents that stretched on as far as Rose could see in both directions. About the center of the camp sat a tent nearly twice the size of the others. The soldier led them there.

They left the horses outside, and with Taurin carrying Maury in a sling attached to his chest, they all went inside.

The man sitting at the desk looked up, then back at the papers before him, then up again, straight at Rose. His mouth fell open and stayed that way for several seconds before he spoke. "Your Majesty? I... I don't understand."

Rose smiled. "It's rather a long story. But be assured, we will get into Legerdemain, with your help or without it. And be assured also that any attempt to stop us will be seen as an act of war upon our royal

145

person, and we will retaliate. Your army will be annihilated, and you with it."

"We're already at war," the prince said.

Rose shook her head. "The treaty Legerdemain has with Kirland is invalid, signed by an imposter. We have no quarrel with you. Legerdemain remains, as it always has, neutral in political matters."

"Even if what you say is true, it doesn't matter. You're here, and cannot control your country. The treaty stands, and thus so does the war. Moreover, you have just handed yourself over to me as my prisoner of war."

Rose narrowed her eyes. He was right, but she couldn't admit that. "War will do your people no good. There is a reason why Legerdemain has been independent for hundreds of years. With the mountains to the north and the forest and river encircling everything, the country is defensible. You cannot attack without your men being slaughtered."

The prince crumpled a sheet of paper in his fist, but his voice remained calm. "You're under siege."

Rose laughed. "A siege will not work, because we are self-sufficient. Moreover, winter is nearly upon us. Have any of your men ever experienced a northern winter? I can see just by walking through your camp, you're ill-equipped for the blizzards that will sweep through this valley, whereas with the mountains and trees to shelter us, Legerdemain is protected from the worst of the storms."

The prince started to open his mouth, but Rose went on before he could say anything. "Moreover, as you say, the treaty with Kirland stands. Even now, their armies are on their way and will attack from the west while Cadalania will attack from the east and Legerdemain from the north. You will be defeated, with no place to retreat but the way you came, empty-handed or even dead. The imposter will not care that I am your prisoner. If you kill me, you only strengthen her hold on my country and your own demise. Your only hope for a peaceful outcome is for me to get into Legerdemain and nullify the treaty with Kirland."

"I will discuss it with my advisors." The prince nodded toward the soldier who'd escorted them in. "Take them to the prison tent until I come to a decision."

Rose held her hand, palm out, toward the soldier. She drew magic through the amulet and created a barrier that prevented the soldier from moving.

146

"No," she said quietly.

The prince stared at her. "What?"

"We will not be your prisoners. We are going to Legerdemain. Now. Your choice to either help us or hinder us will determine whether you will be our ally or our enemy hereafter."

The prince sputtered.

Rose turned and walked toward the door of the tent. The strain of holding up the magical barrier sapped her strength, but she couldn't let it show.

She whispered to Taurin as they walked. "Take Maury. Get on your horse and ride northwest as fast as you can. They'll be guarding the bridge due north of here, but there's a ford half a mile west of the bridge where you can cross."

"Don't just stand there, get her!" the prince shouted from behind them.

Rose pulled more magic and added heat to the barrier. The soldier screamed as his flesh burned every time he tried to push past. Rose felt his pain through the spell and winced, but she couldn't stop now.

She pushed Taurin out the door and untied his horse while he scrambled onto its back. She divided the flow of magic just a little to create a defense around Taurin and Maury, a bubble that would dissipate in a few minutes, but should keep them safe until they were out of the camp.

"Go, now! Keep Maury safe. I'll meet you in the forest."

Taurin charged through the camp, scattering soldiers as they jumped out of his path. Rose whirled around to face the prince and the soldier as they attempted to push through the barrier out of the tent.

Rose pulled still more magic through the amulet, drawing on the energy from in the air around her, the weeds in the camp that hadn't been trampled, all the way to the grasses and shrubs in the field beyond, strengthening the barrier and intensifying the heat.

She couldn't hold it much longer, and she definitely couldn't hold it once she got on her horse to flee.

She just had to maintain it long enough for Taurin to get Maury safely away.

With one hand still holding the shield, she used the other to dig in her cloak pocket for the packet of herbs she'd tucked in there. Holding the packet with one hand, she took a deep breath.

Taurin's horse was well beyond the edges of the camp now. Out of range of bowshot.

In one swift motion, Rose shoved the barrier from her, allowing it to dissipate with a bright flash and a loud pop directly in front of the prince, pulled herself up onto her horse, and flung a handful of herbs—a confusion spell—on the prince and soldier.

She urged her horse to run, the two spare horses in tow. She scattered more of the potion on the soldiers along the way. It wouldn't last long, not dried herbs flung at random, but it would disorient them long enough for her to get within the border of Legerdemain.

Counterspell

Maury began to cry as the horse galloped over the rough ground. Taurin held the boy tightly to keep him from getting jostled as much possible, but that proved nearly futile.

"Just a little more, son," he murmured.

He fought the urge to go back for Rose. She'd made it clear on their long journey that Maury was the most urgent priority, above herself, above her kingdom. As much as he hated the idea of leaving her behind, he knew she'd never forgive him if he endangered their son. More, she wouldn't be able to defend herself if she was concerned for Maury. And she could, apparently, take care of herself just fine.

He'd seen his wife use magic before, of course, but only for Healing. The power she'd wielded to stop that soldier—he'd never even dreamed she'd be capable of so much. He'd thought he knew her, despite her secrets, but he only now realized just how much she'd kept from him, not just of her past, but of herself.

He admired her all the more for having so much power at her fingertips, but not using it for her own gain.

The river lay just ahead.

Taurin slowed the horse a little and rode west, looking for the ford Rose had told him would be there.

A glance behind assured him he wasn't being chased, and he slowed more, examining the river.

There, just ahead, there were no rocks or bends, where the river widened and the current slowed.

He urged the horse into the water, slowly, carefully, out into the middle of the river. It was deep but not strong, and before long, he emerged on the other side, into the forest that grew right up to the water's edge.

The sun was getting low, and Taurin's legs were cold where they'd been submerged in the river. He could only imagine how uncomfortable the horse must be. Rose had told him they'd be safe in the forest, so he led the horse a little further in, out of sight of the river, and found a small clearing to make camp.

He bounced Maury and played with him until he was calm, then set him down and gave him a piece of bread to chew on while he built a fire and cared for the horse.

"Mama?" Maury said after a little while.

"Mama's coming," Taurin said, hoping it was true.

He fed Maury little pieces of meat and vegetables, then bundled him up in a blanket and sat close to the fire until Maury drifted to sleep. He laid the baby down on a bed of blankets near the fire, but not too near, and paced the small camp.

Where was Rose? How had she ended up so far behind him? Something must have happened to her. If she didn't arrive within the hour, he'd…

He'd what?

There was nothing he could do, at least not until he found a safe place for Maury. But who could he trust in a country where he knew no one, and where Maury's life would be in danger if anyone knew his identity?

A noise in the forest jerked his mind back to the present. He pulled a dagger and crouched, ready to attack.

Someone stumbled into the clearing.

Taurin's breath rushed from his body, his relief was so profound. "Rose." He scooped her into his arms and held her tightly. "What happened? Are you hurt?"

"Maury," she said.

"He's fine." Taurin pointed to where Maury's golden curls poked out of the top of his blanket.

Someone else emerged from the shadows of the trees.

Taurin whirled, shoving Rose behind him, and drew his dagger again.

It was an old woman, leading three horses.

No, not just any old woman. The old woman who'd given Rose the amulet. And not just any horses, their horses. Taurin eyed her warily.

"It's all right," Rose said. "She's here to help."

The old woman—Ada, if Taurin remembered correctly—handed Taurin the reins. He took care of the horses while Rose settled in next to Maury and Ada put a pot of water over the fire and threw some herbs in it.

When it boiled, Ada poured the concoction into two cups and handed them to Rose and Taurin. "Drink. This will give you strength. You'll need it. The next few days will be very difficult."

She was right.

The next day, the four of them traveled into the heart of the country. Mountains lined the far horizon. The northern border. It was so small, this country, yet so valuable.

They spent the night at a tavern in the South Village.

"Such imaginative names your people have come up with," he teased Rose.

Rose smiled. "There are only four villages. One in each direction, with the palace in the very center. The palace grounds are like a small city, with shops and artisans in the houses inside the walls, and just around the outside, but most of our country is farmland. The four villages have always just been called by the name of the direction they are in relation to the palace."

She tucked Maury into the little bed, then came to sit on Taurin's lap. Ada sat in the other chair in front of the fire in the room they'd rented.

"The South Village is the largest, because that's on the only trade route out of the country," Rose said. She leaned her head against his chest. "I need to get to the palace first thing in the morning. I'll need Ada to help me with the magic I'll need to reveal Myrta. Which means I'll need you to stay here with Maury."

Taurin shook his head. "I'm not letting you go alone."

"I won't be alone."

"Rose, please. I can't stay here worrying that you're dying. Besides, what if you need the kind of protection that requires a sword instead of magic?"

"I'll stay with the boy," Ada said. "Your husband is right. He should be with you. I can show you how to undo Myrta's spell."

Taurin watched Rose's face twitch as she thought through the proposal. Finally, she nodded. She looked at Ada. "If something happens to me…"

"I will care for the boy until he is old enough to claim his birthright. Your son will be king one day."

Rose breathed deeply, her chest rising and falling against Taurin's. "Very well, then. Taurin, you should sleep while you can. Ada, show me the counterspell as quickly as possible. We leave at dawn."

Taurin lay in the bed next to Maury, but he didn't sleep. He watched as Ada and Rose mixed herbs, carefully measuring proportions, whispering incantations, and making the amulet that hung around Rose's neck glow.

"Rose?"

She turned to face him.

"When you see her… will you have mercy on Jyn? For my sake? I know she has wronged you, but she is my oldest friend. She's saved my life more times than I can count. I know you must protect your kingdom, but if there's any way to be lenient…"

She smiled. "I will. For you."

Usurped

"There is news, m'lady."

Jyn turned toward the squire. "Well? What is it?"

"We've received a dove from our spy in the Sunnland camp. It seems there was a woman who broke through their defenses."

Jyn narrowed her eyes. "A woman? And she broke through? How? Why?"

"They said she used magic, m'lady. And…" The squire paused, shifting on his feet. "She claimed to be the queen."

Jyn's throat tightened, as though a noose cinched around it. The queen? Here? Why? And why now?

"Gather Parliament and send for the queen. We must plan our defense immediately."

Jyn ran toward the council room. She stopped when she saw one of the guards in the hallway. "Ready the men," she said, breathless. "We are going to be attacked. There is an assassin coming for the queen."

The guard jumped, then clattered off in the direction of the guard house.

Marckis came around the corner and grabbed her hand. "What? Is that true?"

Jyn nodded and dragged him along with her. "I've called a meeting of Parliament. You should come—this affects you, too."

Within minutes, the council room filled, and the members of Parliament stared expectantly at Jyn.

154

Jyn stood behind Myrta. "I have just received word that we are about to be attacked."

"Attacked?" a grizzled man whose name escaped her stood up. "Is it the Sunnland army?"

Jyn shook her head. "No. It is someone trying to usurp the throne, a single assassin who will attempt to take the throne by force. The queen's life is in great danger." She turned to Marckis. "Your army is close, you said. How long until they can aid in our defense?"

"Three days. Four at most."

"Send a dove. Inform them that Sunnland may not be our only threat. Have them make all haste."

Marckis left immediately.

Jyn returned her attention back to the men and women gathered around the council table. "We must make a plan to protect the queen."

"I don't understand," the grizzled man said. "How could someone possibly hope to usurp the throne? Even if she kills the queen, she must know we'll never just hand over the kingdom to her. Our armies won't follow her, the guard won't protect her, our people won't obey her. Why would she think she has any chance of taking the throne?"

"Because she is the rightful queen," a voice at the doorway declared.

Jyn jerked her gaze to the speaker. A woman in a long, blue dress, her shoulders draped with a purple velvet cloak, stood there.

Rose.

Rose smiled at the grizzled man. "Hello, Colin. It's good to see you."

Colin looked from Rose to Myrta, two women with the same face, and back at Rose. "What is going on?" he demanded.

"She's an imposter!" Jyn shouted. "Seize her!"

No one moved.

"What are you waiting for? We must protect the queen!"

Colin turned a suspicious glare on Myrta. "How do we know which one is the real queen?"

"That's easy enough," Rose said. She pulled a bag from her cloak and pulled out a handful of herbs. She whispered an incantation, then blew the herbs across the room toward Myrta.

The air shimmered and the spell Gorym had used to transfigure Myrta dissolved.

Everyone around the table gasped.

"There, you see?" Jyn said. "She put a spell on the queen. What more proof do you need?"

"She's right," Colin said. "We don't know whether the spell created this appearance or removed the false image of the queen. We need further proof."

Without a word, Rose pulled a gold chain from her neck. On it hung a glowing purple gem.

All the members of Parliament exhaled as one.

"What is that?" Jyn asked.

"Proof," Colin breathed.

Myrta stood slowly. "How dare you," she said.

Jyn clenched her jaw. This was a fine time for the woman to grow a backbone. Still, she was out of ideas. Maybe whatever Myrta had planned would work.

"You abandoned this country," Myrta said. "Defected. Left your throne for someone else to take. What right do you have to now demand to take it back?"

Rose bowed her head. "You're right. I did abandon my country. I thought I was doing what was needed to save it, and as long as I thought it was being cared for by a rightful heir, I was content to stay away. But you have destroyed my country. In under two years, you've undone nearly eight hundred years of history. You've murdered the royal family and bankrupted the treasury. You've made us beholden to other countries and brought war upon us. It is for this that I reestablish my claim."

"You have no claim!"

Jyn stared at Myrta. Rage contorted her beautiful features into a mask of fury, fueled by hurt, turned to hate.

Jyn knew that feeling all too well.

"You left," Myrta said, "and I had to pick up the pieces you left behind. The throne is rightfully mine. Give me the amulet."

Without a moment's hesitation, Rose tossed the amulet at Myrta.

What in Nyn's name?

It couldn't be that easy. Could it?

Myrta screamed.

Smoke rose from her hand clasped around the amulet, but she didn't let go, even as her hand blackened. Her scream grew louder, more intense, but still she clung to the gem.

156

Perhaps she couldn't let go.

The char spread up her arm, along her body, cutting off her screech when it reached her neck. A moment later, Myrta's entire body crumbled into a pile of ash.

The amulet clattered to the table.

Rose walked around the members of Parliament who all sat stone-still, picked up the amulet, and placed it around her neck.

Colin was the first to stand, then kneel before Rose. "Welcome home, your Majesty."

Everyone else in the room did the same.

Except Jyn.

Jyn still stood staring at Myrta's ashes.

"What would you like done with her, Your Majesty?" Colin asked, nodding toward Jyn.

"Nothing," Rose said. "I can't blame her for being an opportunist. I have no quarrel with her, so long as she agrees to leave in peace."

Jyn gulped, but she bowed. What else could she do?

"Very well," Rose said. "Go in peace." She looked around the room. "Everyone may go. I will begin at once unraveling the damage that was done in my absence. Please, bring all the treaties and edicts to my study."

Jyn shuffled out behind the scurrying members of Parliament. She went the opposite direction, down the hall, just far enough to be out of the way. She leaned against the wall, fighting the emotions that warred in her. Not even in Wyllym's castle, knowing her own brother had betrayed her, had she felt so utterly defeated.

"Jyn?"

Her heart stuttered. "Taurin?"

There he stood, as handsome as he'd ever been.

More.

Standing so close she could inhale his familiar scent, smiling at her in that way he had that softened her, no matter how much he upset her.

"Taurin," she breathed.

In that moment, she felt like everything was going to work out.

In that moment, she was happy.

And the next, her world shattered.

Rose came out of the council room. She walked toward them.

Taurin's gaze turned from Jyn to Rose. "Hello, love. I assume it went well."

Rose smiled. "As well as it could have, I think. I see you found your friend."

His friend. Those words were sharper than the knife Jyn carried in her belt. She glared at Rose. "You. You took everything from me. It wasn't enough for you to take him, even after I'd waited for him for fifteen years, but now this. I finally had a second chance to make something of myself, to be happy, and you stole that, too."

Taurin and Rose both stared at her, wearing twin expressions of confusion.

Jyn looked at Taurin. "I loved you. More than you can imagine. She took that from me. Let's see how she likes it."

In one fluid motion, Jyn drew her blade and shoved it into Taurin's heart.

He gasped, staring at her, his eyes filled with pain.

"If I can't have you," Jyn whispered, "then neither can she."

She shoved the knife another inch into his chest before yanking it out and running down the hall.

Behind her, Rose screamed, a nearly incoherent jumble of demands for the guards and begging Taurin to hold on while she Healed him.

Jyn left the cacophony behind and ran for the dovecote. She almost trampled over Marckis. Grabbing his hand, she pulled him toward the servants' stairs. "We have to leave. Now. The queen is dead, and the usurper is coming for us. We have to get to your army. We have to prepare for war."

The Future

"Send a dove to the Sunnland army," Rose told the squire who awaited her orders. "Request a meeting."

The empty hole in her heart sucked all the passion from her words.

How could she have let that happen? She should've arrested Jyn immediately. She should've insisted Taurin stay behind with Maury. She should've...

How could Jyn have done such a thing? Taurin had trusted her. He'd trusted her with his life, and she'd taken it. Betrayed him. Betrayed *them*.

Rose should've known.

Jyn helped Myrta take over the kingdom. There was another thing she hadn't seen coming. Myrta, her faithful friend, abandoning her and taking her place. How could Rose hope to be a good queen when she read people so poorly? She shouldn't have been so trusting. Shouldn't have believed Taurin when he'd said Jyn was his oldest, most trusted friend.

Rose wiped a tear and tried to focus on the paper before her. Another edict she had to nullify. This one conscripted every able-bodied man into working one day a week clearing out the riverbed so ships wouldn't scrape on rocks in the shallow areas and fords.

The last one had called for "volunteers" to dig new mines—but every family had to send at least one volunteer or pay a stiff tax.

160

Most of these ideas had to have been Jyn's. There was no way sweet Myrta could've come up with them.

A knock at the door interrupted her thoughts.

"Enter."

A soldier poked his head in. "The guards have returned with Ada and the child, Your Majesty."

Rose's heart leapt. "Send them in."

Ada shuffled in, Maury on her hip. He squirmed when he saw Rose. "Mama!"

Ada set him down and Rose pushed her chair back from her desk and held out her arms for him to toddle into. She scooped him up and held him close. "My son. My sweet boy."

Her body shook, but she held back her sobs. He wouldn't understand, and she didn't want to frighten him.

"The soldiers told me about your husband. I'm so sorry, Anarosia," Ada said.

"Just Rose."

Ada smiled. "I'll make note of it for your coronation, Queen Rose."

"Thank you. It needs to be soon. It will take time to send out word that the edicts Myrta put into place have been nullified, but I have already begun. Our more pressing concern is the threat of war. Myrta was married to the crown prince of Kirland. Now that she's dead, and since she was never actually queen, that treaty won't hold, so I cannot expect help from them if Sunnland attacks."

She rubbed her temples with her fingertips. "Cadalania is allied with Kirland, but I don't know if they will want any part of a war. Sunnland initiated war on the grounds that we broke a treaty, but we never actually had a treaty. That didn't seem to matter to their prince, however."

She buried her face in Maury's curls and squeezed him. "If I'd never come back, Taurin would still be alive. But if I hadn't, my kingdom would be dead."

Her eyes clouded with tears as she looked up at Ada. "Was there anything I could've done differently? Any way I could've changed events so they didn't turn out exactly as I Saw?"

Ada sat in a chair on the other side of the desk. "No. You cannot change the future. After your first vision, I tried to See what you had Seen, but instead I saw two paths opened up for you. One choice

161

would've guaranteed your personal happiness at the expense of your kingdom, and the other would've given hope to your kingdom at great expense to you. However, the path was cloudy, and the choice that seemed most unselfish is the one that would've turned out far worse."

"So I could have chosen differently. But how is that possible if I couldn't change the future?"

Ada adjusted her seat and leaned forward. "At the time, it seemed as though there was a choice, but you Saw the future. Seeing isn't like other magic. It opens a window, either to the present or the future, but those events are set, as firmly rooted as the past. Seeing shows only what will be. Therefore, when I Saw the two paths before you, it was the truth of what you had to face, but you Saw what would actually be."

"I don't understand. Why did I have two choices if it was already set that I would make one?"

"The future is unwritten. We must all make our own choices, to the best of our abilities. Yet the Creator knows those choices, and knows the futures before us. I cannot explain it fully, but though the outcome was written, the choice was still yours to make."

"It doesn't make sense. Why are we shown the future, if there is no way to change it?"

"We are not shown a glimpse of the future to try to stop it—stopping it is impossible—but only so we can prepare for it."

Rose rubbed her head. "But it didn't matter what choice I made. One way or another, what I Saw would've come to pass."

"I believe so, yes. So, while your choice set events into motion to come to pass the way they did, the vision still would've come true, one way or another."

"Then why bother at all?" Rose wiped away a tear.

"Because you still had to make a choice. Our choices change us, even if they don't change certain things about the future. One thing I do know, though, is that despite everything, the choice you made was the right one. Dark times are coming. Not in your lifetime, but in his." Ada nodded toward Maury. "And not just his, but beyond his. If you hadn't met Taurin, Maury wouldn't have been born, and it is because he exists that there is hope for the future."

Rose squeezed her son again. It didn't ease the pain of losing Taurin, but she rejoiced that she still had part of him in their son, and that he held the key to her country's future.

Another knock shattered the stillness of the room. "Your Majesty, the prince of Sunnland has received your letter and has agreed to parley. He requests to meet you on the bridge over the river at dawn."

Parley

Rose read the message the soldier handed her from Prince Tristyn of Sunnland, asking for parley. "Send word we agree. Then prepare a small contingent of soldiers to accompany me, and a larger one to secure the border just inside the forest, in case of deception."

When Rose arrived at the river, Prince Tristyn stood on the bridge with a single attendant, though his entire army stood ready on the far bank.

Rose glanced at the general of her army. He nodded to indicate they were ready.

She took Colin with her to the bridge. As the head of Parliament, he'd seen the details of the political quagmire Myrta and Jyn had created.

"Greetings, your Highness," Rose said.

Tristyn bowed his head. "Majesty."

"Thank you for meeting with me. As I mentioned in my letter, the usurper who controlled Legerdemain has been ousted, and all her treaties nullified. We have no desire for war with you. As I mentioned at our last meeting…" Rose paused and allowed the amulet on her chest to glow faintly as a reminder. "We remain, as always, neutral in political conflict."

Tristyn smiled. "Surely you must appreciate my position, Majesty. Usurper or not, your previous queen made a treaty, then broke it and allied herself with our enemy. You can't undo that damage just by claiming the treaty was never valid in the first place."

Rose suppressed a sigh. "What recompense does Sunnland feel is due?"

"A renegotiation of the peace treaty, including a marriage between the royal families which will stipulate that any heir will inherit the throne on Sunnland's behalf. An agreement that Legerdemain's army will come to our aid in case of war. Exclusive access to Legerdemain's waterways."

"Impossible. Such a treaty would be no different from simply handing you the kingdom."

"We could just take it by force."

"You could try." Rose pulled a little bit more magic into the amulet, just enough to make it shine with iridescent light.

Tristyn took a step back, but lifted his chin. "You're about to be at war with Kirland. You can't fight both of us."

Rose raised an eyebrow. "Can't we?"

She hoped the thundering of her heart couldn't be heard, hoped the panic that welled up inside didn't show on her face.

"We would be willing to negotiate a different treaty. Peace between our nations. Access, though not exclusive, to our waterways. But we remain neutral in political and military campaigns."

"Not good enough. We will insist upon a marriage and an alliance in war."

"I have no one to offer you. I am the last of the royal line, and I'm already… I'm not in a position to marry at this point. And there will be no alliance in war."

"A betrothal, then, between one of your children and one of mine."

Beside her, Colin coughed.

"Please excuse us," Rose said. She walked to the far end of the bridge and erected a small magical barrier to prevent eavesdropping. "What is it, Colin?"

"A marriage would be advisable, Your Majesty," Colin said. "It would mean peace for many generations. Providing, of course, the throne remains sovereign to Legerdemain."

"I'm not betrothing Maury to a child from an enemy nation who isn't even born yet."

"I didn't mean Maury."

165

Rose clenched her jaw but didn't answer.

"With respect, Majesty, despite your good intentions, the prince is correct. Your leaving had consequences. If you are to make things right, you may have to do things you don't enjoy."

Rose took a deep breath. "You're right. I will make it happen."

She lowered the barrier and returned to the center of the bridge. "We will agree to a marriage between myself and you, on the condition that you become Legerdemanian, adopting our culture and traditions. Legerdemain will remain sovereign to itself, independent and politically neutral, and any children that result from our marriage will be Legerdemanian and subject to Legerdemanian custom and law of inheritance."

"What of a war alliance?"

"I insist upon neutrality in future conflicts. However, I will agree to give Kirland to Sunnland when we win the war with them, providing you will back us up. Not fight with us, just keep your army here so Kirland has no escape route except through you."

They spent the next half hour negotiating terms and conditions, modifying and compromising as they went along.

At last, Tristyn nodded. "We agree. I will have my advisors draw up the treaty, and yours can read it to ensure the terms are in accordance with our agreement."

Rose curtsied, then both walked to their own sides of the bridge.

"I think that is the best we could've hoped for, Majesty," Colin said.

Rose nodded. "I know. I'm glad it's done. Now I only have one more war to fight."

War

Kirland didn't return Rose's dove.

They didn't send an emissary. They didn't try to negotiate or come to an agreement or even make a declaration.

They simply attacked in the night.

Rose's scouts informed her that the full force of Kirland's army had invaded the country, crossing the river wherever it was shallow enough to do so, avoiding the Sunnland army to the south and concentrating their march along Legerdemain's western border, into the forest.

Rose's army had scouts and small outposts camped in the forest, prepared, but not enough. Rose immediately sent reinforcements into the forest to meet Kirland's army. Though her forces were small, they had the advantage of familiarity with the woods. Kirland's squadrons were struck down almost as soon as they entered the forest, yet they kept coming, pushing further and further into the interior of the forest, a seemingly endless parade of them waiting in line to cross the river as soon as the men in front of them had gone, then cutting their way through the forest, each one going a little further than the last before Legerdemain could cut them down.

Little by little, they gained ground, pushing Legerdemain forces back.

Rose read the latest message from one of her army's commanders, then looked at Colin. "They've realized how much of a disadvantage horses are in the woods. Cavalry are dismounting after they cross the river and proceeding on foot, sending the horses back across the river to carry men and supplies."

"How do you wish to proceed, Majesty?"

"Send men to the dams and tell them to wait for my dove. Keep some troops in the forest to slow them down as much as possible, but assemble the bulk of the army along the plains just outside the tree line, ready to attack any forces that make it through the forest. I'll meet them there."

Rose dressed in armor and settled the amulet carefully around her neck. She kissed Maury, then turned to Ada. "Take good care of him until I return."

The old woman nodded. "As I have always done, for every royal child in this family for generations."

Rose surrounded herself with her personal guards and rode to join her army at the inside edge of her country's border.

Just after dawn, a messenger arrived. "Your Majesty, the remainder of the Kirland army will be across the river within the next two hours."

"And the prince?"

"He has not been sighted."

"Should we send the doves to the dams?" Colin asked.

"Not yet."

"What are you waiting for?"

"Confirmation."

It seemed like a decade, though in reality it was closer to an hour, before the messenger returned. "We have confirmation, your Majesty. The prince is within our borders. He's traveling with a small squadron, using the road as a guide but sticking to the forest. They'll be through the forest soon."

"Excellent."

Rose wrote a message, the same sentence on two pieces of paper.

Open the dam.

She attached each to a dove and sent one to the northeast corner of the country and the other to the northwest.

"Have all our troops pull out of the forest and join us here except for the squadron closest to the prince. Have them monitor his progress, but don't kill him. Be ready."

Rose and her guard rode east, toward the road, and waited.

169

A short time later, a group of Kirland soldiers broke through the trees and stopped at the sight of the Legerdemain army stretched out before them. They formed up ranks but didn't attack.

They had to know that attacking in small groups as they emerged would mean being overwhelmed. Their army would be decimated a little at a time before they had a chance to assemble on the battleground.

So they stood, staring across the field, waiting for direction.

A short time later, a messenger hailed Rose. "He's coming. He should emerge right there." He pointed toward a section of the forest.

Rose and her guard waited just beyond where the prince would emerge. A few minutes later, Prince Marckis and his men stumbled out of the forest.

Jyn was with him.

A flash of violet light from the amulet echoed Rose's anger.

Marckis and Jyn stopped and stared at her.

Marckis looked confused. "Anarosia?"

Rose shook her head. "I don't know what lies Jyn told you, but the woman you married was not Anarosia. She was an imposter, set up to be Jyn's puppet. She is dead, and I am the rightful queen. As such, I am willing to forget the present hostilities and allow you and your army to leave in peace. All except the traitor and usurper, Jyn."

Jyn whispered something to Marckis.

Marckis looked at Rose. "I think you're misunderstanding the power dynamic here. I'm not leaving."

Rose looked at him, willing her voice to remain calm. "You have now forfeited your chance for a peaceful exit. However, I will still accept your surrender."

Marckis actually laughed at that. "What in Kir's name makes you think I would surrender?"

"Any minute now, you'll receive word that the river is flooded. Any of your men still crossing have been swept away, and it is too deep to cross. Your retreat has been cut off. The only way out is across the bridge, right into the camp of the Sunnland army, who are our allies."

Marckis glanced at Jyn and she nodded. "It doesn't matter. I happen to know that my army still outnumbers yours, nearly five to one. I will take this country by force."

Rose allowed a sneer to curl her lip. "She may have set herself up as our ruler, but she knows nothing of our ways, or our defenses. Your army is depleted by more than half, and as you can see, we can easily destroy your forces as they come out of the forces. Surrender now or you will be destroyed."

Jyn snarled and lunged. Two knives slid from her hands and flew through the air, straight toward Rose.

Rose pulled magic through the amulet and aimed her hand at the knives.

A bolt of violet light shot from the amulet, sending the daggers twirling back the way they came, straight into Jyn's chest.

Jyn's face contorted in spasms of hate and pain as she fell to her knees, then toppled over.

Marckis stared at her for a fraction of an instant before raising his sword above his head. "Charge!"

His army swarmed from the forest, circling around him, rushing toward Rose's.

Using the amulet, Rose shot bolts of purple flame at the oncoming soldiers, cutting them down in swaths as they attacked.

Her army, mounted, trampled the Kirland soldiers who were still on foot, slashing them with swords and maces.

Rose pressed forward, toward where Marckis stood gaping as his army was demolished.

She created a magic barrier around him, binding him tighter than any ropes could have, and had him placed on a horse.

At the sight of their captured prince, those who were not dead or hiding in the forest surrendered.

In less than half an hour, the battle was over completely, and Rose sent word that any who surrendered peacefully would be allowed to return to their homeland without further consequence.

Rose summoned a messenger. "Go to the Sunnland army. Tell my betrothed I have a wedding present for him." She nodded toward Marckis.

Marckis's face blanched. "Your betrothed? Please, Majesty, you can't turn me over to him."

"I gave you plenty of opportunities to end this peacefully. You chose this fate, not me. I have protected my kingdom, and now I want nothing more to do with you."

"Majesty, please! You don't know what he'll do to me—to my country!"

"Nor do I care. Legerdemain remains, as it always has, politically neutral."

One Month Later

Rose surveyed her image in the large mirror. Her silk gown and elaborate hairstyle far exceeded the splendor of her first wedding, yet the day held no joy for her. Once the treaty had been signed and Prince Markis handed over, Prince Tristyn had behaved as any man might, sending flowers and expensive gifts, and writing lengthy letters.

Despite the way they had come together, Rose believed he was a good man. In time she might even come to care for him, and his wisdom and experience would certainly be beneficial in ruling the kingdom. She would never stop mourning Taurin, but she would be a good queen, and her country would live in prosperity as long as she was alive.

She reached out for Maury, who sat on the bed beside her. "Come, my son, my heir. It's time to meet your new father."

Dear Reader,

Thank you for reading **The Prophecy**. This story began as a collection of short stories that I published on the blog I write for, New Authors Fellowhip (newauthors.wordpress.com). I had no idea when I first wrote *Rendezvous,* the first story in *The Heir*, that I would grow to love this world so much and that the story would grow into what it is today.

This book marks the halfway point in what I have planned for *The Amulet Saga.* I hope you'll join me for the rest of the journey.

If you enjoyed this story, please tell a friend. Better yet, buy them their own copy.
You can purchase <u>The Heir,</u> and <u>The Defector,</u> and <u>The Silver Shores</u> on Amazon.
Please also check out my first full-length novel, a supernatural thriller called <u>The Breeding</u>!

I love connecting with readers. Please find me on Twitter (@avilyjerome), Instagram (@avilyjeromebooks), my website (<u>www.avilyjerome.com</u>), and Facebook (<u>https://www.facebook.com/AvilyJ?fref=ts</u>).

Yours truly,

Avily Jerome

About the Author

 Avily Jerome is a writer and freelance editor. She spent five years as the Editor of Havok Magazine. Her short stories have been published in multiple magazines, both print and digital. She has judged several writing contests, both for short stories and novels, and she is a book reviewer for Lorehaven Magazine.

She loves all things SpecFic and writes across multiple genres. She is also a writing conference teacher and presenter, and she enjoys speaking to local writers' groups and going to SFF cons.

She is a wife and the mom of five kids. She loves living in the desert in Phoenix, AZ, and when she's not writing, she loves reading, spending time with friends, and experimenting with different art forms.

You can find her on her social media and on her website, at www.avilyjerome.com